Choosing America's Next Superstar

JEFF ERNO

Dreamspinner Press

Published by
Dreamspinner Press
5032 Capital Circle SW
Ste 2, PMB# 279
Tallahassee, FL 32305-7886
USA
http://www.dreamspinnerpress.com/

Choosing America's Next Superstar

Cover Art by Justin James
dare.empire@gmail.com

ISBN: 978-1-61372-759-1

Printed in the United States of America
First Edition
September 2012

eBook edition available
eBook ISBN: 978-1-61372-760-7

ONE

"WHAT are you doing?" his mother asked, standing behind him in the doorway with her hands on her hips.

Embarrassed, Corey spun around and tossed the extension cord to the ground. "Nothing!" he said. "Um, I don't know... being silly, I guess."

"Baby, don't stop," she said. "Your voice—it's beautiful."

At six years old, Corey had never sung before an audience. Well, at least not a solo performance. In preschool and kindergarten, and even in church, he'd sung with the other kids. It was when he was alone in his bedroom that he stood in front of the big mirror, and belted it out. He imagined himself on stage in front of a cheering crowd as he held his microphone. The mic was actually an extension cord with a big block plug on the end. He held it in front of his mouth the same way the performers did on TV.

His mom slipped into his room and sat on the bed, waiting for him to continue. "Go ahead, Corey," she encouraged him. "Please...."

For a brief moment he hesitated, but then dismissed his fear. How would he ever be able to sing in front of a real audience if he had stage fright performing for his own mother? He picked up his microphone, squared his shoulders, and took a deep breath. Then he began to sing a capella. His song choice, "Moon River," was one of his mother's favorites. He knew because he often heard her humming the melody while doing the dishes, and Corey knew every single word.

As he stood there in the center of the room, moving his arms animatedly and maintaining eye contact with his audience of one, he crooned the soothing lyrics to his mother. By the second verse, she was reaching up to wipe the tears from her cheeks.

"Baby, you gave me chills," she said. "When did this happen? When did you get this gorgeous, beautiful, *perfect* voice? Honey, you are amazing! You… you have a gift."

He smiled at her proudly and shrugged, and then started right in on another song. Corey knew a lot of songs. He knew songs from many different genres of music. In fact, he didn't know why, but he could pretty much hear a song one time and remember it. Not only did he remember the lyrics, but in his head he could hear every single note. At age six, he didn't yet know what pitch was, but soon enough he would. Before long, he'd be used to hearing about his "perfect pitch."

With it just being the three of them—his mom, his sister, and himself—Corey's family didn't have much money. Private voice lessons were not an option, but he did participate in every musical activity available to him at school. In high school, he joined choir, drama club, and band. He entered the competition for the school's annual talent show and won first place during his junior year. As a senior, he came in second place, losing only to a silly comedy sketch performed by the high school jocks.

Corey often performed at his church, both as a soloist and a choir member. He sang the gospel songs and hymns with as much passion and sincerity as he conveyed when singing rock or country. Everyone who knew Corey told him how talented he was.

Corey couldn't count the number of times admiring fans suggested to him that he try out for the *Superstar* talent show. That was what everyone called it, but "Superstar" was actually an abbreviation for the internationally popular reality music competition that was officially titled *Choosing America's Next Superstar*. Contestants from all over the country entered the competition every year, and it was the most watched program on television. Millions of viewers tuned in every week to watch the performances of the contestants and then voted on their favorites. They used their cell phones and laptops to cast their votes, and it was the standing joke that more people voted on *Superstar* than in presidential elections.

The dream of being America's Next Superstar was about as distant to Corey as winning the lottery. So many people tried out for the competition every year—tens of thousands—and there was only one winner. The show traveled around the country with its panel of celebrity judges and held auditions. Mobs of people showed up to try out, and only a handful were chosen from each location. The lucky winners were then flown to New York where the elimination-round show was recorded. The four hundred contestants that had been selected from around the country competed for forty top slots.

At last, when the celebrity judges selected the top forty, the judges made one final round of cuts, paring the number by almost half. These twenty-four contestants were the finalists who would fly to Hollywood to perform on live broadcasts for the general public. Viewers were allowed to vote, casting their ballots via phone lines, text messages, or the Internet. The ten competitors who received the most votes during the first week would remain. The celebrity judges would select three other "wild card" contestants from the bottom fourteen, affording them a second chance. After the top thirteen were selected, their fate was in the hands of the voting public. The person with the lowest vote total each week was eliminated, until only one Superstar remained.

Superstar was Corey's absolute favorite television show, and every year he watched it with rapt enthusiasm. He got to know every one of the contestants—he felt like he knew them personally, and he allowed himself to get emotionally invested. Sometimes he selected a contestant to identify with and prayed with all his heart that they would win, then he'd use his computer to vote for them numerous times. It was sort of a way for him to live vicariously through them. He imagined himself as a contestant on the show. He couldn't help fantasizing about what it would feel like to get up on stage and perform for the entire world like that.

When one of his favorites was voted off, it was devastating to Corey. He would feel depressed and almost go into mourning thinking about the fact that when he turned on the television the next week, they would no longer be there. He hated seeing these dreams shattered, and he couldn't imagine what it would be like to get that close and suddenly have it all ripped away.

Corey's family lived in rural northern Michigan, not near any major cities. When Corey graduated from high school, he chose to attend the local community college, not yet sure what to do with his life. He couldn't think of any career he wanted to pursue that did not involve music, but it was just such a long shot. People constantly told him how impractical it was—how unlikely it would be that he'd make it big enough to actually be considered successful. Even his mom, who believed in him with all her heart, advised Corey to choose a path that offered him guarantees. She wanted him to succeed as a singer but more or less told him that his fantasies of stardom were pipe dreams.

So Corey began his freshman year at community college, still living at home. He worked a part-time job as a cashier in a supermarket and lived a lifestyle that was not atypical of a college-aged American kid. He hung out with friends, went to parties, and did all the things most other kids his age did.

"Did you see this?" Megan whispered. Corey and Megan had been best friends since eighth grade. They were in the college library, and she had her laptop open. She turned it so he could see the website she had open.

"Yeah, I know," he said, a little too loudly. He looked around to make sure he hadn't disturbed anyone. In a quieter tone, he went on. "The Detroit auditions are next week. I'm scheduled to work... plus how would I even get down there?"

"I'll drive you!" she said. "Dude, you can't pass up this chance!"

He shook his head, sighing. "Meg, if I lose this job, I'm screwed. I can't just blow off my schedule for this one-in-a-million chance. Do you know how many people audition for *Superstar* every year?"

"Fifty-seven thousand," she said matter-of-factly. "It says so right there in the article."

"Exactly! And out of that many auditions, they only pick four hundred. And out of the four hundred, only *one* person wins."

"And that one person is *you!*" she said with enthusiasm. Now she was the one raising her voice.

"Shh," he said, holding up a finger to his lips. "Thanks, Meg… but it's just not possible. But, hey, I promise to watch the show with you every night." He smiled at her and winked.

Shaking her head, she grabbed him by the wrist. "Listen to me, Corey Dunham! You are *not* going to pass up this opportunity! You're going to call your boss right now and tell her you need the time off. Say it's an emergency. Say you had a death in the family. Say anything you need to! But one way or another, I'm dragging your ass to that audition. You have the most beautiful voice I've ever heard."

"Megan, please…."

"No! Don't 'Megan, please' me. You're doing this."

He pushed his chair back, leaning backward so he was balancing on the back legs. "Okay. I'll think about it. I'll see if someone can switch with me, but if it comes down to choosing between my job and the audition, I can't lose the job."

"It won't. Seriously, there are, like, a million kids that work there. They can find someone to cover your shifts."

"We'll see," he said. He smiled as he thought about the possibility. "But what will I sing?"

MEGAN, who usually wore her long red hair in a bun, was letting it down on the road trip to Detroit. With all four windows open, she and Corey cruised the interstate at 85 mph, the stereo blasting. Corey was so thankful for his best friend, and he couldn't begin to express how much he appreciated the faith that she had in him and his talent.

As per Megan's prediction, it all had worked out. When Corey told his boss about his chance to audition for *Superstar*, she was quick to rally the troops and get his shifts covered. Janine was actually his department manager, and she was a huge fan of *Superstar* herself. She made Corey sing a song for her in the office and was moved to tears.

"You're gonna make it!" she exclaimed. "Oh my God! I can't believe one of *my* employees might be America's Next Superstar!"

When Corey informed his mom that he was headed for Detroit, she was not quite as optimistic. "Oh, baby, you know I'm proud of you. I just don't want you to be disappointed. There are so many people who try out every year. You know I believe in you, but I'm a realist."

"I know, Mom," he said. "I won't get my hopes up too high. But can you imagine if...."

"You listen to me! No matter what happens, you will always be *my* superstar."

In a way Corey was sad that his mom didn't want to go with him to the audition. He understood, though. She had to work. It also would have completely changed the dynamic of their road trip had his mother accompanied them.

Corey was riding shotgun with his feet propped on the dashboard, and they spent almost the entirety of their five-hour drive singing and listening to the stereo. Of course, Corey already had his audition song picked out, and Megan forced him to sing it to her at least a dozen times, critiquing him with brutal honesty.

They'd always been this way in their relationship with each other. Corey could tell Megan anything without fear of judgment, but he also appreciated the fact that she was always going to offer her honest opinion. He could accept criticism from her in ways he couldn't from any of his other friends or family. He was quite self-conscious, and a lot of times, when people said mean things to him, it hurt his feelings. He knew when Megan said something critical, she wasn't being harsh. She was simply speaking her mind.

That type of relationship was extremely valuable to Corey. He could trust Megan and knew she'd never lie to him. When he bought new clothes, got a new haircut, or even started crushing on a new guy, Megan would tell him exactly what she thought. Corey felt as if he'd always been out to Megan. There never was a big coming-out scene. She'd just always known.

There were a lot of other people in Corey's life that were in the dark about his sexual orientation. He'd told his mom and sister, and he had a few gay friends from high school. At work it wasn't really an issue. Male coworkers would sometimes talk to him about girls, assuming that he was straight, and Corey didn't feel the need to correct them. He'd simply listen and nod. With a lot of straight dudes, the idea of a guy being attracted to another guy was so foreign to them that the notion of gay coworkers never entered their mind. Unless it was a girly guy, swishing and sashaying across the room making passes at them, they'd just assume that the dude was heterosexual.

Corey was not exactly what you'd consider a masculine guy himself. He wasn't flamboyant—didn't go around snapping his fingers all the time and flopping his limp wrists in front of everyone—but he definitely related emotionally to girls more than to guys. His best friend was female, after all. He liked the sappy romantic-comedy movies that everyone called "chick flicks." He loved shopping and fashion and romance novels. He never accepted the theory that men and women were just wired differently and that their thought processes and feelings were diametrically opposed. If that were the case, then why was it that he could always understand and relate to the girl's point of view more than the other guy's?

The auditions were being held in Detroit at Ford Field, the indoor stadium that the Detroit Lions used for their home games. The most challenging thing was finding parking.

"Holy fuck, look at all the people," Megan said. Contestants were lined up outside the stadium entrance for what looked like at least a quarter mile.

"Oh my God," Corey said, suddenly feeling very small and insignificant. "I don't think this was such a good idea."

"What do you mean? You have just as good a chance—no, *more* of a chance—than any of these people. I bet half of them couldn't carry a tune if it had a handle on it."

"Meg, I probably won't even make it through the interview process. How can you expect them to get through all these people in just two days?"

She rolled her eyes exasperatedly. "Corey, you gotta have a little faith. Once they hear your voice, they'll be blown away." She pulled into a parking lot that had a "$10.00 Parking" sign. She rolled down the window and paid the attendant, who then directed her to park at the end of the line.

"Well, I'm glad we brought our cooler," Corey said. "I think it's gonna be a long wait in the hot sun."

"It'll be fun," she said, a little too much cheer in her voice. "You'll see. We'll make lots of friends."

Corey didn't doubt that. Megan had a very outgoing personality. Her gregariousness allowed her to easily strike up conversations with complete strangers. There were times Corey wished he could be more like his best friend, and he especially envied her eternal optimism. Meg was always upbeat and happy, and she always seemed to see the glass as half full.

As expected, once they were in line, Megan began chatting with those around them. One of the other contestants in line was a punk rocker named Jeremy from Toledo. "This is my third year," he explained.

"Really?" Meg said. "So what's it like?"

"This here's the worst part. You wait in line for hours just to get an interview."

"But you've been through it before," Corey said. "What happened?"

"First year, I never even made it to the preaudition," he said. "They cut me before ever even hearing me sing."

"Really?" Corey couldn't believe it. "How could they cut you without even knowing if you had talent?"

Jeremy laughed. "Dude, this isn't about *talent*. It's about show business. It's reality TV. They're looking for a mix of interesting people who'll mesh together in a good drama. That's why you see all the shit auditions every year. They deliberately let in some really suck-ass singers—a lot of them are obviously horrid—just to make an entertaining reality show."

"And they pass up a lot of genuine talent?" Megan asked.

"Exactly. There are only so many spaces."

"So what do we have to do to make it through the initial interview?" Corey asked.

"Anything unusual. If you have a sad story to tell, that's a biggie. Talk about your humble background. Tell them you're living under a bridge or in a tent, that you're homeless. Tell them your mother died when you were five, and you're doing this so she sees you from heaven. Tell them you have cancer...."

Corey's mouth dropped open. "Seriously?"

"Dude, I'm dead serious. My second year I gave them a hard-luck story about how I was estranged from my father who was a drug addict and going through rehab. They ate it up."

"But you didn't make it all the way...."

"I made it to New York, and was voted out during the group performances. I got stuck with the lamest group of the competition. It totally sucked."

"And what about last year?"

"I didn't even get through the first interview. That was in Cincinnati, and I got there too late. They'd already filled all the spots."

"What are the judges like?" Meg asked. "Is Reuben as mean in person as he is on TV?"

"Reuben doesn't know jack," Jeremy said, laughing. "He has virtually no musical talent himself. He couldn't tell you if someone had pitch or not. To him, it's all just showmanship. He's the mastermind behind this whole scene. He says humiliating shit to people because it makes an entertaining show. Like I said—drama."

"So what's he really like then?" Corey asked.

"I never really talked to him one on one other than in the audition. He made fun of my hair and said I needed a makeover." Corey could believe it. Jeremy had a fluorescent green Mohawk, and he was totally right about Reuben. He was a complete asshole. He made fun of everyone and offered very little constructive advice.

"My favorite judge is Krystal," Megan said.

Jeremy laughed. "Yeah, everyone likes her. The girls like her 'cause she's sweet, and the guys just like her tits. Half the time she's either drunk or stoned."

"Really?" Corey asked. "I always thought she was the best judge."

"You do realize that the celebrity judges are not the *real* judges...."

"What do ya mean?" Corey asked.

"It's a *show*!" he exclaimed, holding his hands out for emphasis. "The producers of the show 'consult' with the judges before they make their final cuts. Even during the auditions, the so-called judges are wearing earpieces. They're actors, doing what the show tells them to."

"Is the voting at least real?" Corey asked. "I mean, after they begin broadcasting the live shows."

"Supposedly," Jeremy answered. "Who knows. I think it's probably pretty much legit. But everything prior to that point—all the auditions and various rounds of competition—that's all rigged. The producers are looking for a mix of contestants who will make a great entertainment show. It has very little to do with musical talent."

"Damn," Corey said. "What the hell am I even doing here?" He turned to Megan. "I don't have a sob story or anything...."

"What are you talking about?" she said, slugging him on the shoulder. "You have an awesome sob story. Tell them about being raised by a single parent who worked all her life in a factory. Tell them how you knew from the time you were six that you wanted to be a singer."

Jeremy guffawed. "Dude, that's *everyone's* story."

"Maybe," Megan said. "But not everyone can tell the story the way I can. I'll have them bawling their eyes out. I'll tell them how Corey won the talent competition in high school and told everyone how he felt his dad looking down from heaven...."

"I never said that—"

"Yes, you did!"

"Megan, my dad is still alive!"

"They don't need to know that," she said. "And you don't have to lie... let me do it."

"You might have something there," Jeremy said. "Don't worry, everyone lies about shit to get on the show. If they don't at least fib a little, they don't even make it in to the auditions."

"But don't they eventually find out?" Corey asked. "I mean, the show. Don't the producers find out these stories are bogus?"

"Eventually. They don't care either. Like I said, it's all fiction. They're just putting together an entertaining show. If you're lucky enough to make it through the auditions, then you can set everything straight with the media when they start hounding you for interviews. It's all just part of the game."

"So let me do the talking," Megan said. "You just stand there and look pretty."

"Meg, they probably aren't gonna even let you into the interview with me...."

"You'll see when we get in there," Jeremy said. "There'll be chairs set up everywhere. After you fill out your application, they'll give you a number, and then they'll come around and interview you right where you're sitting. After that, you just wait and hope they call your number."

"How long do you wait?" Corey asked.

"Till they say it's over. You might be waiting until tomorrow night...."

"Oh, man, that sucks!" Corey complained.

"We won't be waiting that long," Meg said with confidence. "You watch. You're gonna get your audition... or I'm gonna die trying."

THREE hours later, when they at last made it into the auditorium, it was as Jeremy described. On the main floor, there were tables and chairs set up. Corey took an application and began filling it out. Meg snatched it from him and took over.

"I'll do it," she said.

"At least let me see what you're writing… so I know when they question me."

"Don't worry about it," she said. "Like I said, I'll do the talking."

After completing the form, she jumped up and stepped over to the cubicle where the applications were collected. She had to wait in line for about five minutes and then returned to Corey. "Okay, now we go over here to these chairs and wait for them. Here's your number." She was holding a big white label with red print. It had the number 748 on it. "You wear this like a necklace," she explained, sliding the rope over Corey's head.

"Wow," he said. "Like a beauty pageant or something."

"Or a marathon."

Corey pulled out the small cooler from under his seat and grabbed a bottle of Diet Coke. "Want one?" he offered Megan.

For the next hour, they waited as the chairs around them filled up. Corey glanced around him to see if he could spot any other contestants being interviewed.

"They're over there," Meg said, pointing to one of the female contestants. "And she's number 722, so it won't be much longer."

"Do they only have one person interviewing?" Corey asked. "That's crazy."

"I think they have one per section. We're in the seventh section which is why our number is in the 700s. When they get up to 799, they start over with the numbering."

"God, it's taking long enough," Corey complained.

"This is nothing," another contestant said. Corey turned to see the boy seated beside him. "I hear that the real wait comes after the interview. That's when we have to go camp out in the audience section and wait to see if they call our number for an actual audition."

"Yeah, we heard that," Corey said. "Have you been through this before?"

The kid shook his head. "Nah, it's my first time." Corey looked down at the guy's number, and it was 781.

"I'm Corey," he offered. "Aka, number 748."

"Jimmy, number 781," the dirty-blond kid said, smiling. He looked to be about Corey's age but a little better built. Corey couldn't help but notice his muscular chest. He was wearing a navy colored T-shirt and jeans, and he had a bit of a Southern accent. "Where are y'all from?" Jimmy asked.

"Up north... do you know where Petoskey is?"

He shook his head. "Nah, I'm from Kentucky... northern Kentucky."

"Is this the closest audition for you?" Corey asked.

"They had one in Louisville, but I missed it," he said. "My brother was having surgery that day."

"Really? Is he okay?"

Jimmy shrugged. "I hope so. He was born with a rare heart condition. This is, like, the sixth operation, but they say he's doing pretty good."

"Aww, wow." Corey suddenly felt a pang of guilt for the sob story he knew Megan was planning to tell on his behalf. "You should tell them about your brother," he said. "I mean, when they interview you."

"You think so?" Jimmy asked. "Why would they want to know that?"

"I dunno. I just think it's a touching story, how you almost missed your chance at an audition in order to be with your brother. Is he older than you?"

"He's two years younger. We always been close, though."

"Well, I'll keep him in my thoughts," Corey said, smiling sincerely.

"Thanks, man. You know what you're gonna sing?"

"Yeah, I think so," Corey said, "if I'm lucky enough to get an audition."

"I'm singing Garth Brooks," Jimmy said. "'The Dance'."

"Oh, I love that song. I like a lot of country, but I'm gonna go with a boy band song. 'Shape of My Heart' by the Backstreet Boys."

Jimmy started singing the chorus to the song, smiling at Corey. "Lookin' back on the things I've done…."

"I was tryin' to be someone…," Corey finished.

They both laughed. "Cool, so you know a variety of stuff?"

"I love all kinds of music," Jimmy said. His chocolate-brown eyes seemed to light up as he smiled at Corey. "What about you?"

"Yeah, I guess I'm the same way. I have this knack for remembering song lyrics. If I hear a song once, I've pretty much got it in my brain."

"Me too… I thought I was the only one like that."

"Do you know this one? 'When superstars and cannonballs are runnin' through your head'," Corey started singing.

"'Television freak show, cops and robbers everywhere'," Jimmy continued.

Corey cracked up. "Dude, you have an awesome voice!"

"You too, man."

"This is my best friend, Megan," Corey said. He thumbed his fist in her direction, but she was busy talking to someone else and had her back turned.

"I came alone," Jimmy said. "It was a five-hour drive."

"That's almost exactly how long our drive was, but we never left our state. Weird."

"Hey, maybe we'll get lucky and both make it through," Jimmy said. "We can hang out together."

"I'd like that," Corey said.

"Are you number 748?" a voice said from the other side of him. Corey quickly turned to see an official-looking lady carrying a clipboard.

"Yes! That's me," he said, jumping up from his seat.

"Corey Dunham?"

"Yes, ma'am, that's me."

"I'm Renee, and I conduct the preaudition interviews."

"I'm Corey's best friend Megan." Corey heard his companion introduce herself. "I'm the one who brought him here."

Renee shook hands with both of them. Looking around, she located an empty chair and pulled it over in front of them. "Well, let's just talk for a few minutes. Tell me about yourself, Corey, and why you want to be America's Next Superstar."

"Forgive me," Megan blurted out before Corey could open her mouth. "Corey is a little bit shy when it comes to talking about himself, but he has the most amazing story."

"Oh?"

"Corey has a brother—two years younger than him—his name is Jimmy, and he has a heart condition." Corey's mouth dropped open in shocked disbelief. Megan must have been eavesdropping on his conversation. "Jimmy and Corey are very close, and Jimmy just had to have a life-saving surgery. Corey wasn't even going to come to the audition, but Jimmy insisted. He told Corey to go and win his way to New York. Corey's doing this for him, his dying brother."

"Wow," Renee said. "Has he been ill for a long time?"

"It was a condition he was born with, and they didn't expect him to even live this long. Jimmy prays every day he will be able to hang on long enough to see his brother crowned America's Next Superstar."

"Amazing, that's truly a touching story," Renee said. "You know...." Her voice was beginning to choke up. "You know, I think we're going to just go ahead and put you through to the auditions. Corey, why don't you come with me?" She stood up and grabbed Corey by the arm.

"But…." Corey turned and looked at his new friend Jimmy, who was just sitting there with a dumbfounded expression on his face.

"Go ahead!" Megan urged him. "Corey… go!" Megan stood up and grabbed Corey's other arm.

"You come with us," Renee said. "They'll need to film Corey's supporters. Are you with him too?" she said as she turned to Jimmy.

"Uh… no. I have *nothing* to do with him," Jimmy said, quickly turning away.

Corey felt his face redden. Suddenly he was being escorted across the huge auditorium floor toward an area that had been cordoned off with large collapsible walls. They were like huge cubicles. Corey assumed that this was where they did the actual filming.

"Wait here," Renee said. "I'll be right back."

Corey turned to Megan. "Oh my God! I can't believe you just did that."

"Did what?" Megan said, as she grabbed Corey and spun him around. Suddenly he was staring directly at a television camera. "You mean that I told the touching story of your dying brother? Corey, you shouldn't be shy or embarrassed by how close you are to Jimmy. He's *so* proud of you."

Corey looked up into the camera and gulped, suddenly unable to speak.

Megan wrapped her arm around his shoulder. "Don't you worry. I have so much faith in you, Corey Dunham… and so does Jimmy."

The next thing Corey knew, someone had stepped up beside him. Corey's jaw just about came unhinged when he turned to see it was Dylan Seagraves, the host of *Choosing America's Next Superstar*.

"Corey, I've heard your story… our producer just chatted with me. It's very moving. Can you tell us what you're feeling right now?"

"Um… I'm a little nervous…."

"I can understand that. It must feel like you have the weight of the world on your shoulders right now. If you don't do well and make it through the audition, you're going to feel as if you let your brother down. This may be your very last chance to make this dream a reality for him...."

"Uh... yeah."

"He gets very emotional about this," Megan said. "Surely you understand...."

"Oh, of course," Dylan said, nodding emphatically.

Just then Renee stepped up behind them. "Okay, Corey, do you happen to have a photo of your brother?"

"Uh... no."

"We've got lots of pictures we can bring you," Megan volunteered. "I might even have one in my purse. It's locked in my trunk...."

"Good," Renee said. "Regardless of what happens with the audition, we'll want those photos. We can get them later, though. This show won't be aired until several months from now. Corey, I see your song choice is 'Shape of My Heart'. Does this have any significance to your brother?"

"It's his favorite group," Megan said. "Corey sang him this song just before he went into surgery."

"Mmm, very good," Renee said, jotting down notes on her clipboard. "Okay, Corey... usually you'd sing in front of one of our voice coaches before going on camera, but we've decided to go with this... whether you can sing or not."

"He can sing—"

"Doesn't matter," Renee interrupted. "He has the look, he has the story... that's all that matters."

"But...," Corey began to protest.

"They're ready!" Dylan said. "Time to go in." He grabbed Corey by the shoulders and spun him around, pushing him toward the door.

"But what do I...?"

"Just march right in there. They'll tell you what to do."

Renee grabbed Corey by the arm and led him through the door and down a long hallway. When they reached the end, she stopped.

"Here," she said, handing him the papers from her clipboard. "Give these to the gentleman right over there." She pointed to a man who was wearing a headset. "He'll give your paperwork to the judges, and they'll call you when they're ready."

Corey took a deep breath and grabbed the papers. He stepped forward, into the next room. When he got up to the man Renee had pointed to, he held out the papers. The man turned and placed his finger over his lips to indicate silence. He glanced at the papers and nodded, then pointed to a bench, indicating Corey was to sit.

He could hear the activity in the next room. It was an audition, and the contestant was embarrassingly flat. It was a male singer, and he had a serious pitch problem. Corey couldn't tell exactly what the judges were saying, but there were shouts followed by laughter. After a few moments, the contestant stormed off the stage into the room where Corey was waiting. He was dark haired and skinny, and at this point he was obviously crying. He didn't stop to say anything to either Corey or the man with the headset. He just marched right on by.

"Okay," the man said, turning to him. "You're next. Wait here till I come back."

The man disappeared, stepping out of the room onto the stage. About thirty seconds later he was back. He waved his hand, motioning for Corey to stand. "When the green light comes on, they're ready for you." He pointed to a light on the opposite side of the stage. "Sometimes the judges take breaks in between contestants. Sometimes not. You just have to wait here."

Corey nodded. "There's a problem with…."

"You're on!" the man said, shoving him out toward the stage.

He stumbled at first, then righted himself. Taking a deep breath, Corey willed himself to place one foot in front of the other. When he looked up, he was center stage, standing directly in front of the four judges he'd seen thousands of times on TV.

"Hey there," Raymond said. He was the heavy-set rap singer whose trademark was his dark sunglasses and excessive bling. "Who do we have here?"

Corey swallowed hard, and then forced a smile. "Corey... uh... Corey Dunham."

"Nice to meet you, Corey," Krystal said. She was smiling broadly.

"Thank you," Corey said, looking at each judge. It was all so surreal. He felt as if he were dreaming. There they were, all four of them. Reuben, Krystal, Tyler, and Raymond. He knew all about them—or he thought he did. He'd watched them on the show since he was a little kid.

"And where are you from?" Reuben said with his thick Australian accent.

"Here in Michigan, sir. I'm from a small town in the northern part of the state."

"So lots of snow," Tyler said. "Do you ski?"

Corey tried to look cheerful, smiling again. "Yeah... a little bit."

"And why are you here?" Raymond asked. "You're gonna be America's Next Superstar?"

"Uh... yes. Yes, definitely!"

"Very good," Reuben said. "I like your confidence. But let's see if you can put your money where your mouth is. What are you singing today?"

"'Shape of My Heart' by Backstreet Boys," Corey said.

Reuben rolled his eyes and Krystal smiled sweetly at him. "Very well, go ahead," Reuben said. He crossed his arms obstinately, waiting for Corey to start.

Corey was very relieved they didn't ask him about the story of his nonexistent, fatally ill brother. He took a quick breath, straightened his posture, and began to sing. As he belted out the notes, his entire body was infused with confidence. Right from the first bar, he knew he'd nailed it, and the melody flowed out of him with intense emotion.

All four judges sat there, staring at him. Corey made it all the way through the first verse and chorus before Tyler raised his hand and indicated for him to stop. "Holy fuck!" the aging rock star exclaimed. "Boy, you can *sing*!"

Corey smiled, proud yet a little self-conscious. "Thank you, sir," he said meekly.

"You gave me goosies!" Krystal squealed, holding her arms out to show her goose pimples.

Reuben nodded, a very serious expression on his face. "Very well, shall we vote? I say yes."

"Yes," Raymond quickly added.

"Definitely yes," Tyler said.

"Corey, you're going to New York!" Krystal exclaimed. She held out a sheet of orange-colored paper. "Here's your golden ticket."

"Yes!" Corey shouted, pumping his fist in the air. "Oh... oh... oh! I can't believe it!" He stepped down from the stage to take the paper from Krystal. "Thank you. Thank you so much!"

As he turned, he saw the man with the headset waving frantically, motioning for him to exit through a different door. Apparently winners had to go out the opposite side of the room than the losers did. He thought it would be like on television, that he'd be dashing outside to wave around his ticket to Dylan and Meg, but instead he was led down the hallway to an office area.

"Congratulations," a slender middle-aged female said as she greeted him. "Have a seat." She introduced herself as Ms. Warren. After sitting behind a desk herself, she pointed to one of the empty chairs, which Corey slid into as per her instruction.

Ms. Warren then proceeded to ask him a series of questions including his name, address, and phone numbers, and if he had any health issues. She explained that he would be mailed an airline ticket to New York, be provided transportation and hotel accommodations, and a return flight in the unfortunate event that he was voted off during the competition. This was all for the pretaping. The elimination process would all be conducted during the first two weeks of September. They would begin with approximately four hundred contestants, but only about forty of them would make it through all the elimination rounds. If he did happen to be one of those lucky forty, he'd then have to fly to

Hollywood in January and would stay there for the duration of the live broadcasts.

Had he been under the age of eighteen, he would have been allowed the accompaniment of one parent or guardian. Being that he was eighteen, this did not apply. He would be completely on his own.

"Do you have any questions for me?" she asked.

"Uh... yes, ma'am," he said.

She smiled sweetly. "Okay, go ahead."

"Well, it's not really a question. It's more like a confession...."

"Oh?" she said, leaning forward in her chair.

"My friend who's with me—Megan—she told the producer some things about me that weren't true."

"What kind of things?" she asked, still smiling.

"She gave them a sob story, saying my brother was dying. I don't even have a brother, though."

Ms. Warren started laughing. "Aren't you the sweetest little thing? Honey, don't worry. Everyone has a sob story. It's all part of the game. You should thank your friend for her creativity. Did you look out there and see the tens of thousands of kids all tryin' to get on this show? If they didn't have some kind of story to tell, they'd never make it."

"But what about my audition? I mean, they filmed me and asked for pictures of my brother...."

"When you can't produce the pictures, they just won't air that segment. But you know what that means? It means from this point on, it's all about your talent. I heard you singing in there, and you're good. Focus on that."

"Oh... thank you. Thank you very much."

"Now you're gonna take this golden ticket with you. Don't wrinkle it or fold it. But you'll go right out this door. One of the production crew workers will then take you over to the filming area where they'll have you exit through a door and film it as if you're leaving the stage and running out to reunite with your family members."

"Really? That's how they do that?"

Again she laughed. "Yeah, it's different than how it appears on television."

"But the families always act so surprised."

She nodded. "Showbiz."

"Okay… well, thank you so much. I guess this is it, then."

"Congratulations, honey. You have a good time in New York. And good luck."

TWO

"I'M NOT going," Jimmy insisted. "It's too soon."

"You're going or I'm gonna get out of this fucking bed and kick your lily white ass!" Charlie said, a serious scowl wrinkling his brow.

Jimmy couldn't help but smile at him, biting his lower lip so as not to burst into laughter. "Bro, don't worry about it. We can talk about it later. Right now, you just need to concentrate on getting better."

"Dude, you don't have the luxury of time. If you don't leave for Detroit within the next few hours, you're gonna miss your chance. And if you blow this because of me, *I* will never forgive you. You promised me...."

Jimmy sighed as he looked into his baby brother's eyes. "Yeah," he admitted, nodding. "I did promise you, but I didn't know at the time that you were gonna need open-heart surgery."

"That was a week ago, and now I'm doing fine. You already missed the audition in Louisville because of that. You can't use that excuse again. If you really wanna do something to make me happy, you'll get in that piece of shit car of yours and hightail it to Detroit... and win *America's Next Superstar*."

Jimmy stepped over to the bedside and ruffled his kid brother's hair. "You have a temper," he observed.

"Damn right," Charlie agreed. "Dude, I swear to you I wouldn't be like this if I didn't know you have the most awesome voice in world. Everybody knows it. Everyone who's ever heard you."

"You know, there's always next year...."

"There might not *be* a next year for me."

"Charlie, don't say that."

"It's true, and you know it. They didn't expect me to make it this long. Is it too much for me to ask you to at least try? Can't you do that much for me?"

Jimmy felt his throat tighten. He didn't want to break down in front of his brother, so he just nodded. After a pause, he responded. "No," he whispered, "that's not too much to ask. I'll do it for you, Charlie."

"Good. Then get moving!"

Jimmy leaned in and wrapped his arms around his sibling. He took extra care not to squeeze him tightly because of the incision, and Charlie slapped his back in a manly sort of way.

"Well, then... I guess I better get home and start packing."

"Text me when you get your golden ticket," Charlie said.

"You know I will."

"RENEE, get in here!" Reuben was shouting into his phone. "Where the hell are you?"

"Gimme a minute. I'll be right there."

It had already been a long morning, and the day was only half over. Reuben didn't know how many more annoyances he could tolerate. The string of contestants they'd paraded before him and the panel of other judges had been incredibly disappointing, to say the least. Sure, some had been good. Some were amazingly talented, but that wasn't what interested Reuben.

As the team broke for lunch, Reuben stepped down the hallway into the executive suite where he'd be having his lunch. These were the suites that typically were reserved by dignitaries and big-shot corporations when they wined and dined their guests at the football games. Reuben took a seat in one of the secluded offices and waited for his assistant, Renee, to arrive.

"Reuben," she said, gasping for breath as she stepped through the door a few seconds after their phone conversation, "what's up?"

"What's *up*?" he repeated back to her, his voice dripping with sarcasm. "I should be the one asking you this question. I specifically told you what I was looking for this morning, and so far you've only delivered one decent-looking male contestant."

She looked him in the eye and shrugged. "I'm sorry, but I can only work with the people who show up to audition. Do you want me to go out on the street and round up some young twinks for you…?"

"I don't care what you have to do, but you know as well as I that the reason this show's been a huge success is because every teenage girl in America tunes in to vote for their favorite heartthrob."

"And I suppose the fact that you get the perk of fucking their cute twink asses has nothing to do with it."

Reuben's mouth flew open in mock astonishment. "Why, I've no idea what you're insinuating," he said with a grin. He was holding his hand over his chest as if truly offended.

"Yeah, right," she said, rolling her eyes. "Reuben, don't worry. I'll get you plenty of pretty boys to drool over. I snatched that one right up this morning. I knew he'd be your type, but when you keep bitching at me, it doesn't make my job any easier."

"Who was that kid, anyway?" Reuben said, ignoring her complaint.

"Some hick from the boondocks. Petoskey or something. Wherever the fuck that is. I guess his brother's dying of cancer or heart problems or some shit. Made a good sob story, plus he had the look."

"Well, make a note. I want to make sure he makes it through the elimination rounds."

"Got it," she said. "You gonna eat?"

"Grab me a sandwich or something," he said as he slid his laptop onto the table in front of him. "And anything with alcohol. Scotch, preferably. Actually, eighty-six the sandwich and make the scotch a double."

"I'll get you a sandwich and a Diet Coke," she said. "One drunk on the judges' panel is plenty."

Reuben sat down and fired up his computer, surfing immediately to find a porn site that featured young blond males.

JIMMY'S interview had not gone so well. He tried explaining to the lady that he was the one whose brother was in the hospital after a critical heart surgery, but she just wasn't interested. She said they already had that angle covered. He then tried explaining to her that he'd been singing all his life, and everyone he knew encouraged him to try out for *America's Next Superstar*.

She'd smiled sweetly. "Very well, then, if you want to take a seat, we'll call you when we're ready for your audition."

This was the same line they used on everyone. Jimmy couldn't believe that Corey kid, the way he'd chatted with him and pretended to be his friend only to steal his story. He'd always known there were people like that—people who would do anything they had to do to get ahead regardless of who they walked on—but it had still surprised him when it happened.

As he sat there, he texted Charlie and told him he was now waiting for his audition. He didn't bother explaining that he would actually be lucky to even get one. All he could do at this point was wait.

And wait he did, for the next several hours. It was after five o'clock when it became obvious that a lot of the contestants were beginning to clear out. After waiting all day, many were giving up on the idea of being called. Jimmy would wait until they closed up shop for the day and then go try to find a safe place to sleep. He couldn't afford a hotel room, but he also couldn't drive all the way back to Kentucky.

Finally at five forty-five, just as he was starting to doze off, he heard his number.

"Seven eighty-one. Number seven eighty-one."

"Oh my God!" he shouted. "That's me! That's me!"

He gathered up his things and quickly headed out onto the auditorium floor. He dashed over to the reception desk and informed them they'd called his number. Just then, the lady who'd interviewed him stepped up.

"Oh yes... good. Very good. I wasn't sure if I called the right person. I remember talking to you and was hoping I matched up the right name with your face. You're the cowboy."

Jimmy beamed at her excitedly. "Yes, ma'am. That'd be me."

"All right, come with me. Do you have anyone with you?"

"No, ma'am," he said.

"Well, then I'll have you store your things in one of these lockers. We would normally have you go before a voice coach for prescreening, but we are pressed for time. You had a good story and the look we're after, so we're going to just send you right on in to the actual judges."

"I do? I have a good story? I thought you said you had that angle covered...."

"Oh... well, we can never have too many good stories." She smiled at him, her voice sugary sweet.

"Well, that's okay, ma'am. I told ya I can sing, and I can. You won't be disappointed."

"Now that's the spirit," she said.

Five minutes later, Jimmy's knees were knocking as he stood offstage waiting for the green light. When it finally came on, he hurried across to the center of the platform and looked down at the judges. His heart pounded in his chest as he took in their familiar faces.

Reuben looked up and gave him a sly grin. "Hello, young man. What is your name and why are you here?"

"Hello, sir," Jimmy said. "It's a pleasure to meet y'all. My name's Jimmy Sawyer and I'm here to become America's Next Superstar."

Tyler began laughing. "Jimmy Sawyer. You related to Tom Sawyer?"

Jimmy chuckled obligingly at the lame joke. "No, sir. Not's I'm aware of."

"And what are you singing today?" Reuben asked.

"'The Dance' by Garth Brooks."

Krystal gave him the cue to begin, and he did, all the while thinking of his kid brother and the promise he'd made to him.

Thirty seconds later, he was on his way offstage, carrying his golden ticket.

"I made it!" he said into his cell phone. He hadn't even waited until he was outside to call his brother with the good news. "I made it, Charlie, and it's all because of you!"

ABOUT a month prior to the elimination rounds, Corey received a phone call from one of the associate producers of *America's Next Superstar*.

"You'll be flying into JKF Airport," she told him. "All of our flights are through American Airlines, and when you go to baggage claim, look for the *Choosing America's Next Superstar* sign. One of our representatives will be stationed there and will get you on a shuttle to the hotel. We have shuttles running every two hours.

"If you are accompanied by a parent or guardian, you'll be assigned a room together. If alone, you will be assigned a roommate.

"All rooms are nonsmoking. All activities associated with *Choosing America's Next Superstar* are nonsmoking. If you are seen to be smoking during any official *Superstar*-sponsored event or activity on or off set, this will be grounds for immediate disqualification.

"Alcohol and drugs are prohibited with the exception of designated, off-camera furlough days during which time contestants over the legal drinking age are permitted to consume alcohol in moderation."

She took a deep breath and then continued. "You will be required to comply with the standards of decency as defined in the handout, 'Choosing America's Next Superstar: Standards of Decency', which will be mailed to you along with an indemnity waiver. Both the waiver and the sign-off for the decency standards must be turned in on the day of your registration.

"Sexual contact with fellow contestants, judges, production crew members, voice coaches, hair and makeup artists, consultants, hotel staff members, transportation specialists, honored guests, wait staff, housekeeping, and any other individual associated with *America's Next Superstar*, is strictly forbidden."

In other words, don't have sex.

"We're also sending you a nondisclosure agreement. Interviews with media prior to the broadcast of *America's Next Superstar* are strictly forbidden. Publicly revealing the outcome of taped broadcasts to the media is a breach of contract and will result in legal action. All interviews with local or national newspapers, magazines, and television stations will require the express written permission of *Choosing America's Next Superstar*. Posting of videos on YouTube or other Internet social media is also prohibited.

"In the event that you successfully complete the elimination round, you will be assigned to a media consultant who will create and maintain a social media presence for you and your celebrity identity. Said consultant will monitor and manage all communication with the general public via the numerous media.

"*ANS* is a reality television show, and you will be required to consent to the filming of any and all activity, conversations, arguments, disagreements, emotional outbursts, or expressions of intimacy. In other words, you will have very little privacy. Refusing to be filmed or to allow camera crew access to you when requested will result in a breach of contract and legal action up to and including disqualification from the competition."

In other words, don't plan on having any *privacy.*

"During the initial elimination rounds, you will be on your own, so to speak. If you make it through, a team of specialists will begin working with you. You'll be assigned a wardrobe consultant, a hair and makeup specialist, a voice coach, a choreographer, a media consultant, and a personal adviser.

"Participation in all scheduled events and activities that have officially been designated as part of the *ANS* itinerary are mandatory. Failure to comply will result in legal action up to and including disqualification."

Corey was beginning to wonder if he was stepping into something that was more than he'd bargained for. He didn't realize there'd be all these rules and regulations. It was so orchestrated, and everything seemed so rigidly planned and controlled.

As if sensing his trepidation, the associate producer paused. "You still with me, hon?"

"Yes… yes, ma'am," he answered.

"I know it's a lot of legal mumbo jumbo. Anyway, everything I've told you will be in the packet I mail you. You should receive the material along with your airline ticket and return-trip voucher by certified mail within the next three days. Try to relax and enjoy the experience. We're thrilled to have you on the show, and we wish you the best of luck. Cary, do you have any questions for me?"

"Um… it's Corey. My name's Corey, not Cary."

She laughed dismissively. "Oh yes, sorry about that. Any questions, Corey?"

"I don't think so. Not yet, anyway."

"Very good. There is a contact number in the packet. If you have any problems with your flight, call that number. If not, we'll see you in September."

"Thank you so much," Corey said.

The night before his departure, Megan threw him a going-away/good-luck party. A group of coworkers, friends, and family members gathered at the bowling alley. Even though Corey wasn't allowed to talk to the media, word had gotten out in the community that he was going to be on *Superstar*, and the local paper had run an article about him. It was weird how already he was beginning to feel like a celebrity.

Megan dragged him into the bar where a local band was playing and convinced the band to let Corey sing. Not used to being in the limelight, Corey was a bit taken aback, but as he took the stage he relaxed and found his voice. The response of the crowd was encouraging, bolstering his lagging self-confidence. He knew he had a big challenge ahead of him. Here at home he was quickly becoming a celebrity, but he'd soon be a small fish in a very big pond. With four hundred competitors all vying for the top slots, he knew the odds were against him, and he prayed he would not return home with disappointing news.

JIMMY'S family rallied around him, as did most of his small-town community. Word of his success during the auditioning process spread like wildfire throughout the county, and Jimmy's phone had been ringing off the hook. Former classmates from high school that he'd barely ever talked to were suddenly friending him on Facebook. People were already making fan pages for him and posting pictures of him from years ago, during his early childhood.

Jimmy also received a phone call from an associate producer at *Superstar*. When she explained the nondisclosure clause, he was concerned.

"But they already talked to me. The paper and the TV station. They came right to the house and it was on the news."

"That's okay," she said. "Going forward, refer all media inquiries to our publicists, and do not talk to anyone about the selection process from this point on."

"Yes, ma'am," he promised.

Jimmy's send-off was a small gathering consisting of close family members and friends. They had a pizza party in his mama and daddy's family room. It felt great being surrounded by so much love and good wishes, and the loved ones who'd gathered were all just as supportive of his brother Charlie as they were of Jimmy. The family had been through so much.

"I'm gonna win this thing for my bro," Jimmy said, holding up his soda can in a toast. "Here's to you, Charlie. I love ya, man."

The next morning Jimmy's parents drove him to Louisville where he boarded his flight at 7:00 a.m. The departure itself was uneventful and rather anticlimactic. This was likely a good thing, Jimmy surmised. His mama was crying, probably due to a combination of genuine pride and anxiety. This would be the first time in Jimmy's life that he'd be away from home for so long.

Jimmy was not ashamed to admit he was a mama's boy. He and his mother had always been very close, and she was the very first person Jimmy had ever confided in about his sexual orientation. It had come as no real surprise to her; she told him she'd always sensed it. Mamas were just that way. They could sense things.

Daddy was another story. Telling him was the hardest, but he didn't take it too badly, all things considered. He gave Jimmy a short lecture about how he loved him no matter what. Maybe it wasn't the most politically correct way for a father to express support of a gay son, but that was just Daddy. He was a man of few words.

Even after Jimmy came out to his family, he didn't flaunt his sexuality. He was a very private person, and he didn't think it was really anyone else's business whom he chose to love. He also didn't think it was true what all the TV shows and movies said about gay people. The famous gay male celebrities all seemed to be so flashy and girly acting. He liked to think of gay men as being more like Ennis and Jack in *Brokeback Mountain*. To Jimmy, that was what being gay was all about. He was a man—a *real* man—and he didn't see why any man would want to go around acting like a woman. That wasn't what he was attracted to, and that wasn't how he wanted to be himself.

It surprised him how much he'd liked that kid at the auditions. Corey. It was too bad the guy was such a conniving, lying little snake, because he was actually kinda sexy. But even Corey wasn't what you'd call flamboyant. He had softer mannerisms but was far from girly.

It didn't matter. There were lots and lots of hot guys in the competition. He'd have plenty of eye candy, but that'd be all it was. Jimmy had already been severely warned about fraternization. Sex of any kind with any of the other contestants or employees of *Superstar* was strictly forbidden.

Seemed kind of weird to him. Every year during the live broadcasts there were always rumors circulating about on-set romances. Two years ago, Krystal had been rumored to have had a torrid affair with one of the Top Forty contestants. It was a great big scandal. And there always were all kinds of stories going around the Internet about Dylan Seagraves. A lot of people said he was gay and took young male contestants home with him to share with his live-in boyfriend.

Honestly, Jimmy didn't care about all those rumors. He suspected most of them were spread on purpose. The old saying was that there was no such thing as bad publicity. As long as people were talking about *Superstar*, they'd be tuning in.

Jimmy knew it would be necessary to keep his private life private. He wasn't about to come out of the closet to the whole world on *America's Next Superstar*. And if he made it through the elimination rounds, it would be all the more important that he conceal his orientation. In previous years, certain contestants who were rumored to be gay had gotten voted off. The general public just wasn't yet ready for an openly gay Superstar... especially not an openly gay *cowboy* Superstar.

THREE

"OH GOOD God, stop the fucking insanity," Reuben whined as his limo pulled up to the front entrance. "Another mob of talentless, moronic wannabes." The fact that these talentless wannabes were the same people who'd made him filthy rich didn't even cross his mind. All he could think about was what a long process it was going to be over the next fourteen days. Four hundred sniveling brats all vying for the coveted top slots, all willing to do just about anything to ensure their secure place in the competition—well, maybe that part wasn't so bad.

Reuben's position as judge gave him tremendous power. And contrary to the naïve beliefs of the general public, he was far more than just a single vote on a panel of four judges. This was *his* reality show. If he chose to have a contestant eliminated, he could make it happen. To simply state that he wanted something to happen would result in his desires becoming reality.

It was a very comfortable position to be in, especially while here in the midst of all these gorgeous teen heartthrobs. Every year since the competition began, Reuben had handpicked his favorite playmates. They were all basically the same. Eighteen to twenty-three-year-olds. Slender to medium builds, not too bulky. Smooth. He liked the all-American, clean-cut look. He liked narrow waists and clear complexions. He preferred blonds with tight little bubble butts and pearly-white smiles.

In past years, some had been crooners, the type you'd see in just about every boy band. Some were beat boxers, some country boys, and some rockers. He didn't much go for the thug, bad-boy look. A couple tasteful tattoos in the right places were okay, but none of that wild hair or grotesque body piercing. What Reuben preferred was purity. He wanted his boy meat to be undefiled and innocent, and most of all— compliant.

How could they not comply with his wishes? They all knew how much power he wielded. If they were not fully aware that he held their fate in the palm of his hand, he could easily make it crystal clear to them. Sure, there had been a few who'd resisted his advances. It wasn't really surprising. Pride often led people to make stupid decisions about their lives. But the smart ones, the ones who truly wanted to succeed, knew better than to say no to him.

If one of the chosen boys was unwilling to submit to Reuben's wishes, he simply eliminated him. There were plenty more where they came from. And there were times when Reuben himself tired of a particular boy toy. After being with him a few times he was no longer undefiled, and it was time to move on to the next one.

His assistant Renee had often scolded him for playing this game. "You're fucking filthy rich," she reminded him. "Just hire yourself an escort. Get yourself a boyfriend and come out of the closet. Get yourself *ten* boyfriends if you want. Reuben, for God's sake, you can have any kind of guy you want—any kind that money can buy."

But that was just it. He didn't want to *buy* sex. He didn't want some prostitute that had slept with hundreds of men. He wanted innocence and purity, and he wasn't just looking for a trophy boy to show off to the world. Reuben had a public image to maintain. He was regarded as an enormously successful businessman and one of the most powerful forces in the music industry. That was what it was really about—power. Renee was right about it being a game. Not only were each of these young men his conquests, but he also held their fate in his hands. He was the ultimate kingmaker, and this gave him an incredible rush.

As he made his way through the crowd and into the building, he headed straight for his dressing room. He placed his briefcase on the vanity, opened it, and removed a manila folder. It contained the headshots of the contestants he'd chosen. There were three in particular who had caught his eye.

Ah yes, Corey Dunham. He'd sung some sappy boy-band ballad. Perfect. He was gonna be a huge hit. Christ, he'd be a star even without his voice. Every teenage girl in America would be tuning in—fantasizing about seeing him shirtless. They'd rush out to buy his CDs and memorize every syllable of his songs. He chuckled as he thought of it. The very thing these teen girls craved the most would be what Reuben himself already had. Staring at the cherubic face of his next teen superstar, Reuben reached down and groped himself. He closed his eyes and tilted his head back, allowing himself to visualize his fantasy.

After a deep breath, he moved on, leafing through the stack of photos. Another one he liked was in there someplace. *Yes, here he is...Jimmy.* Jimmy Sawyer, the country boy. The kid also possessed that same innocence. Although not as refined and soft as Corey, Jimmy was pure. He had a down-home quality to him, and that accent of his, coupled with the deep baritone voice, was exquisite. Reuben imagined the sound of it. He was sure by the time he was done with the boy, he'd be singing at least a few notes a couple octaves higher.

And there were others. Plenty of them. It had been a good season after all. Of the 198 male contestants who had been selected, a good three dozen of them appealed to Reuben's taste. He just had to get through the drudgery of the first few days, let the kids get settled in. Allow them to begin feeling the pressure of the competition—then he'd make his move. And he had already decided which boy he'd go after first.

ALTHOUGH the flight consisted of several passengers who were *America's Next Superstar* contestants, Corey didn't recognize any of these fellow travelers. The two faces he'd hoped to see were Jeremy the punk rocker and Jimmy the Kentucky cowboy, but he had no way of knowing whether or not they'd made it through. Even if they had been successful in their auditions, they were from other cities. Jeremy said he was from Toledo and Jimmy lived near Louisville.

Corey had thought a lot about that Jimmy, and he wondered if the kid's little brother was doing okay. He deeply regretted the tactic that Megan had used to secure Corey's audition, and he was afraid that Jimmy probably pretty much hated his guts at this point. He didn't blame him. Corey hoped that Jimmy was there in New York, and if so, he'd apologize to him.

He had to admit that his interest in Jimmy stemmed from more than just his guilty conscience. From the moment they'd started talking to each other, Corey had felt a connection to him. For one thing, the guy was hot. He was smoking hot, and with his tight Levis and form-fitting muscle shirt, little had been left to Corey's imagination. The guy was built like a brick house, and every brick was in place.

Of course, it made no sense for him to allow his thoughts to head in that direction. He was going to New York for a sole purpose. He was going to focus every bit of his energy and attention on winning the competition. He didn't have time for romantic fantasies. They were a distraction. Besides, fraternization was forbidden. It was right there in the contract in black and white. Contestants were not allowed to become sexually involved with each other or with any member of the *Superstar* staff.

Still, thinking about Jimmy was a difficult thing to avoid. That deep, baritone voice. The broad shoulders and blond hair. Though not exactly the type of guy Corey had always considered himself attracted to, he just couldn't get the Kentuckian out of his head. It was crazy—silly, even. The possibility that Corey would ever see him again was next to nothing. Out of all those thousands of contestants, only four hundred from across the country had been chosen.

"You must be a Superstar." A voice beside him pulled Corey from his pensive state back into the present.

He turned to the girl and smiled. "And you too," he said. "You just have that look."

"So, you from Michigan?" she asked.

"Clear up north. Petoskey."

"Ah, up in ski country. My family vacations there sometimes, at Boyne Highlands."

"I have a friend who works there," Corey acknowledged. "My name's Corey, by the way."

"Sam," she said. "Samantha, officially."

"Nice to meet ya, Sam. Is this your first year?" he asked.

She nodded. "But it's been a dream of mine for as long as I can remember."

"Me too," he said, turning slightly in his seat to face her. "I'm so psyched."

"Psyched and scared shitless. I'm so afraid that after all this anticipation I'm gonna be voted off right away."

Corey sighed, placing his hand on her forearm. "Believe me, I totally know what you're sayin'. There are, like, four hundred of us, and over the next two weeks that number will be whittled down to only forty. The odds of survival are *not* in our favor."

"I just can't think about it," she said. Sam had wavy, shoulder-length auburn hair, and it seemed to bounce when she got excited. Corey thought she should be in a shampoo commercial. "If I let myself obsess on it, I'm gonna go crazy."

"I know," he agreed. "So where are *you* from?"

"Saginaw. Born and raised."

"Wow, my mom has a cousin or something from that city."

"You ever been there?" she asked.

"Nah. I've never been anywhere, actually. This is my first time on a plane. It's my first time out of Michigan."

"Seriously? You've never even been to Cedar Point or Disney World or anything?"

He shrugged and shook his head. "What can I say? My family… well, it's just my mom, sister, and me… we never had a lot of money."

"Well, that explains why you've been staring out that window," Sam said. "First time fliers always do that—look out the window at the clouds and all the little tiny buildings and mountains below."

"Yeah." He smiled at her. "I guess I was kinda obvious. So, ya know, even if I don't make it through the elimination round, I'll always be thankful for the adventure. The trip itself is pretty exciting."

"After this is done, you should come visit me. I'll take you to some clubs."

"Really? I'm not even old enough...."

"Don't worry. I can get us in. There's a really cool gay club right in Saginaw. You ever hear of Bambi's?"

Corey felt his face getting hot. "A gay club? Why you think I'd go to a place like that?"

"Oh, I don't know... because maybe you're, um... gay?" She cracked up. "Dude, you *are* gay, aren't you?"

Corey released a sigh of defeat. "How the heck did you know?"

"Sixth sense," she said. "Half my friends are gay. I can sense it."

"But you're not gay yourself?"

"Fuck no." She lowered her voice. "I love cock too much."

At this point Corey was certain his face was bright crimson.

"You're kinda cute when you blush like that," she said. "And don't worry. Three-quarters of the music industry is gay... at least."

"There are always rumors that Dylan Seagraves is gay."

"Oh, he totally is," Sam stated, matter of fact. "And maybe Reuben. I've heard that rumor too."

Corey made a face. "Ew, I wouldn't wanna think about that possibility."

She laughed again. "Not your type, huh?"

"I don't know. He's just so unattractive to me. I think the fact that he's so mean to everyone just makes him seem ugly."

"I kind of like him," Sam admitted. "I know he sounds mean, but he gives very blunt, honest advice."

"You think so? I think he's half-cocked most of the time. Some of his so-called advice is just meanness. I could see if he offered genuine criticism, something constructive. But what Reuben does is belittle people. He rips them to shreds and tries humiliating them."

"How was he during your audition?"

"He rolled his eyes a couple times, but overall he wasn't too mean. He voted me through."

"Wow," she said. "I wish I could say that. He voted against me, but the other three liked me."

"All that matters is you got through," Corey said, smiling. "And now we all start with a clean slate."

The captain made the announcement that they were preparing to land, and the seat belt lights came on. "Oh, wow, I can't believe we're here already," Corey said.

"Look out, New York, here we come!"

FORTUNATELY, Jimmy was not the only *America's Next Superstar* contestant on the flight from Louisville to New York City. He'd never been to a big city like New York. He found Louisville and Detroit to be challenging enough. When the plane landed and he stepped into the terminal, he just followed along, trailing behind the excited group of fellow contestants as they made their way to the baggage claim area.

He'd never seen such diversity. Thousands of people surrounded him, all different ethnicities, speaking different languages. It seemed odd that so many people shared the same space at the exact same moment and yet didn't even notice one another. Where Jimmy came from, people greeted each other. Being friendly toward strangers was just the proper thing to do. Jimmy had been raised to be mannerly, to always demonstrate hospitality. Those values appeared nonexistent in this city. Everyone just hurried about, pushing and shoving their way to the head of the line. After a mere twenty minutes in JFK airport, Jimmy was already beginning to feel homesick.

At the baggage claim, he spotted the sign for *Superstar*. Relieved that he'd made it that far, he just had to retrieve his two pieces of luggage and guitar from the conveyer and check in with the company representative. As he tried edging closer to the revolving belt, others crowded around him, pushing him back. "Excuse me," he said politely. "Oh, I'm sorry, ma'am, pardon me." Ten seconds later: "No please, after you... go ahead." This continued for the next five minutes until Jimmy realized he was not one inch closer to the luggage than when he'd started. Finally he opted for a slightly less polite approach and pushed his way through the crowd.

He spotted one of his bags on the other side of the belt. He just had to wait for it to make its way around to him. As he stood there, a heavyset traveler reached in front of him, grabbed a large suitcase off the conveyer, and whipped it off the belt. The bag flew into Jimmy's midsection, and he gasped, stumbling backward. The force of the blow took him by surprise, and he flailed his arms as his feet slid out from under him. Suddenly he was flat on his behind amidst a sea of impatient airline passengers who were anything but sympathetic of his fall. "Move it, asshole!" someone shouted. "Hey, you fucking klutz!"

"I'm sorry! I'm sorry!" Jimmy tried desperately to gain some footing and right himself, but with so many people pressed against him, it appeared he was about to be trampled. Out of nowhere, a hand reached down, and he grabbed hold of it appreciatively. As he rose to his feet, his mouth dropped open when all of a sudden he was face to face with the one person he'd hoped to never see again.

"Jimmy, you all right?" Corey said.

"Thanks," he said, pulling his hand away. For a few seconds, they stared into each other's eyes, then Jimmy turned away. By that time, his bag had come around, and he reached down to grab it. Fortunately his other suitcase and guitar case were right behind it. Once he had his luggage, he pushed his way back through the crowd.

"Dude." He heard Corey's voice behind him. "You all right?"

Jimmy spun around. "I'm fine. Thanks for the help." He turned to head toward the Superstar sign.

"Wait," Corey said. "Please...."

Heaving an exasperated sigh, Jimmy spun around once more. "Look, man, I don't really wanna talk to you."

"I know," Corey said quickly, "and I don't blame you. I feel so bad...."

"You *should* feel bad. My brother almost died."

"How is he? Is he doing better now?"

Jimmy couldn't believe the audacity of this kid. Did he actually think Jimmy was going to tell him *anything* about himself or his family ever again? "Not to be rude or anything, but you oughta mind your own business."

"I'm sorry, really I am. I had no idea my friend Megan would do that."

"But you went along with it. You didn't stop her."

"I know." Corey was hanging his head shamefully. He looked up, making eye contact with Jimmy again. "It was an awful thing for me to do, and after I got in there I told them the truth."

"The judges?" Jimmy asked. He found this hard to believe.

"No, the judges didn't even ask anything about it. I'm so glad you made it through your audition. I was worried I'd never see you again. I was afraid I'd never be able to tell you how sorry—"

"Look, man, you said you were sorry. You've got a clean conscience, so can you just leave me alone now?"

Jimmy turned around and headed briskly across the room to register for his shuttle.

"WHO was that guy?" Sam asked him. They were on the shuttle on the way to the hotel.

"Look! It's the Statue of Liberty," Corey said. "I hope we get a chance to see some things while we're here."

"Yeah, I forgot... this is all new to you. But anyway, that guy who fell back at the airport."

Corey sighed, still staring out the window. "Some kid I met during auditions. His brother has a heart condition and had to have like six surgeries. He's from Kentucky."

"He's cute as fuck," she said.

"He hates my guts." Corey turned to her, cocking his head to the side.

"Oh, I doubt that, judging by the way he looked at you."

"He looked at me like he wanted to kill me, and I don't blame him."

"What do ya mean?"

"It's a long story, but things didn't go too well when we met in Detroit. I was hoping I'd see him here so I could apologize to him. I'm just glad he made it through."

"Well, if it's any consolation, it didn't seem to me that he hated you. I couldn't hear what he said to you, but he looked surprised to see you more than anything. I'm sure you'll have a chance to make up with him."

He couldn't help smiling. "Sam, I really don't even know the guy. We just met briefly, and like I said, he despises me. I've gotta stay focused on the competition. I don't have time for that kind of drama."

"Or romance?" she said.

Just then one of the other contestants on the shuttle began to sing "I've got a Golden Ticket," the theme song from *Charlie and the Chocolate Factory*. The shuttle bus was packed, and nearly everyone joined in, including Sam. Corey sat there grinning, thinking about Jimmy with a golden ticket. He joined in on the chorus:

"'Cause I've got a golden ticket. I've got a golden chance to make my way, and with a golden ticket, it's a golden day...."

When they got to the hotel, it was pandemonium. The lobby was bustling with people, all fellow contestants pouring in from the shuttle buses. Corey looked around at all the happy faces, realizing that it would be very soon that the numbers would begin dwindling. Within the first three days, half of the competitors would be eliminated. After that, there would be two rounds of group competition, followed by one final round of solo performances. By the end of the two-week process, there would be only twenty contestants remaining. He looked around at all the people and did the math. Only one out every twenty would survive. It was scary.

He stood in line with Sam, waiting to register.

"You got your paperwork?" she asked.

"Yup," he said confidently, pulling a file folder from the side pocket of his suitcase. He began leafing through the documents. "Indemnity waiver, nondisclosure clause, code of conduct agreement, rights to my first born…."

She cracked up. "No shit. I wouldn't be surprised if they asked for a blood sample."

"Or urine," he said, more seriously. "They could do drug testing."

She guffawed. "God, I hope not. I'll be on the next flight out. Last night I was so freaked about the competition, I smoked a big fat one."

"Really?" he said, laughing. "I never got into it. Weed, I mean. I don't like the taste… or smell."

"Well, I could like use a good buzz right now."

"I know what ya mean, but we can't even drink."

"Bull*shit*," she said. "I read the rules. We can drink… 'in moderation'. And believe me, I'm gonna very moderately get my ass wasted, just as soon as we're checked in." She winked at him.

"Oh, that's right. You're older and more worldly. I'm not old enough to even be served."

"Well, there's such a thing as a liquor store, ya know. I can get us a bottle…."

"We'll see," he said. As much as he liked Sam, he was not about to go get drunk or stoned, especially not on his first night there. Getting through the competition was going to be challenging enough on its own without complicating things. He knew if he were lucky enough to make it through the elimination rounds, there'd be plenty of opportunity for celebration afterword.

When they got to the head of the line, Corey turned in his paperwork and was given a packet containing the itinerary, a name badge, and a voucher for his return flight. He pulled the voucher from his packet and held it up. It looked so ominous, a bleak reminder that he was only one screw-up away from complete failure.

After they'd registered, they had to go to the front desk to check into a room. "I wonder if we'll be assigned roommates," he said.

"Let's see if we can room together," Sam suggested.

"I'm sorry," the desk clerk informed them thirty seconds later, "room assignments have already been made, and we have strict orders not to make changes."

"Oh, come on," Sam pleaded. "Who's gonna find out? There are so many people, they'll never know."

"Oh, they'll know," the dark-skinned male clerk assured her. "All roommate assignments are same-gender. If I put a guy and a girl together, that'd cost me my job."

She rolled her eyes in disgust. "So I'm getting stuck with some chick I don't even know? What's the difference if I room with a girl or a gay guy?" Her voice was getting loud as her tone became more argumentative.

"Sam, just chill," Corey said. "I'm in the same situation... I'll be with someone I don't know...."

"Dude, these rules make no sense. They don't want guys and girls bunking together because of some Puritan bullshit prudishness. But you're *gay!* They're gonna put you with some other guy. The whole thing is so self-defeating. I mean, think about it. You're far more likely to do something naughty and, God-forbid, *sexual* with another guy than with me!"

"Sam, for God's sake, will you shut up?" She was starting to piss him off. Why on earth would she think it was okay to just out him like that in front of everyone?

"Just relax, dude," she said. "You're in New York now. Half the people here are gay. I bet *you're* gay, right?" She turned to the desk clerk. He didn't answer but instead raised an eyebrow.

"Look," he said, "all I can do is give you your room keys. Where you decide to actually sleep is up to you. Perhaps you could arrange a swap or something."

"Well, thanks for nothing... Raif," she said, reading his nametag.

"You're more than welcome, miss," he said with the most insincere smile Corey had ever seen. He handed them their keys, and as he did so winked at Corey. Maybe Sam's gaydar was right again.

JIMMY had never felt so flustered. This whole *America's Next Superstar* thing was starting to seem like a really bad idea. He felt out of his element in the big city with all the huge buildings and noisy crowds. He'd never seen so many cabs. As he sat in the backseat of the shuttle bus, he stared out the window behind him, and all he could see were taxis.

He was sitting next to a rather nerdy-looking kid with spiked hair. The guy was tall and super slender and was wearing headphones. He bobbed his head, humming along to the music. It appeared as if everyone involved with this competition was either rude or obnoxious. Or they were dishonest, like that Corey dude.

Jimmy couldn't believe his bad luck, running into Corey again at the airport. Well, actually, Corey had kind of saved him right when he was about to be trampled. It didn't matter, though. That didn't excuse what he'd done. Back in Detroit he'd pretended to be Jimmy's friend only to use him. Jimmy wasn't about to let that happen again.

As he sat quietly in his seat on the bus, he took a deep breath and looked around. Why was he allowing himself to feel overwhelmed? Why was he being negative? This was the most amazing experience of his life, and he should be celebrating. He should be overjoyed right now.

How many people actually got a chance to live their dream like this? This was no time for self-pity or depression. For all those years growing up, he'd sat in front of the TV, glued to the screen during every episode of *Superstar*. Now here he was a part of it!

As soon as Jimmy got inside the hotel, he called home. "Mama, you wouldn't believe this city. It's so huge… and busy. And there are so many people racin' round here like chickens with their heads off. I ain't never seen nothing like it. … Aw, now, don't you worry. Everything's fine. I just wanted you to know I made it all right. And I'll be home in about two weeks… hopefully not beforehand. … Yes, I love you too. Tell Daddy I love him… and Charlie. Listen, I gotta go. I got to put my bags in my room and meet my roommate. There's just one meetin' tonight for everybody, then tomorrow we start the elimination rounds. I'll call you after I get my results."

Jimmy then registered and picked up his room key from the front desk. He wasn't exactly sure what nationality that desk clerk was, but he sure was cute. Seemed like he was flirting too. Obviously he was not a true New Yorker or he wouldn't have been so friendly.

There was no point waiting for a bellhop. With so many guests checking into the hotel at the same time, they were all running their tails off. Besides, Jimmy just had the two pieces of luggage and his guitar. The one suitcase was a mite bit heavy, but he'd manage. It helped that they had those little wheels on the bottom.

When he got into the elevator and pushed the button for his floor, a young lady slipped in just before the door closed. "Floor eight, please," she said, smiling broadly.

"You from *Superstar* too, ma'am?" he asked. It was kind of a dumb question. She was carrying a registration packet just like his own.

"I am," she said, nodding. "I'm Teri, and you are?"

"Jimmy," he said, holding out his hand. "Pleasure meetin' ya. Where y'all from?"

"LA," she said. "And you must be from Kentucky?"

"How'd you know?" he asked, tilting his head to the side and squinting.

"Lucky guess," she said. "You're a cutie. I knew you must be from either Kentucky or Alabama or Georgia. Somewhere in that vicinity…."

"Or Tennessee," he said. "They talk the right way there too."

She laughed. "Let me show you a little secret," she said. She reached down and pulled up the handle of Jimmy's suitcase. "It's a lot easier to pull your suitcase behind you when you use the handle. Here, let me see your smaller bag." She grabbed it from him and flopped it atop the big suitcase, sliding the strap around the handle to secure it. "See? Isn't that easier?"

"Ain't you smart?" he said. "I guess you can tell I ain't done much travelin'."

"Well, if you need help with anything else, you let me know, cowboy," she said. The elevator bell rang and the door came open. "This is my floor. Good luck!"

Jimmy decided he'd been entirely too hasty in his assessment of the people here in New York. That was the second friendly face he'd encountered in the past five minutes. God must have been smiling on him after all. Now if he could just be lucky enough to end up with a decent roommate….

It took him a minute to figure out exactly how to use the room key. When the desk clerk first gave it to him, he thought it was a mistake. It didn't look like any key he'd ever seen before. Seemed more like a credit card, but when he saw the handle, it all made sense. He had to push that credit card thing into the slot. It took him three tries to get it to work. After his second attempt, he pulled the card out and read the instructions. "Insert this side up and remove quickly. Turn handle when green light appears."

As he stepped through the door, it became obvious his roommate had already arrived. There was a big suitcase on one of the beds and clothes hanging in the closet. Apparently he was in the bathroom. Jimmy thought about knocking and letting him know he'd arrived but wasn't exactly sure what he'd say. He decided instead to take a seat over in the desk chair and wait for his room companion to finish up in the bathroom.

About two minutes later, he heard the bathroom door opening. Jimmy stood up and stepped toward the door. His mouth dropped open when he saw who emerged. Dripping wet and wearing only a towel, it was Corey.

FOUR

"NO WAY!" Jimmy objected. "You are *not* my roommate."

Corey, slightly embarrassed by his seminudity, grinned sheepishly. "Wow," he said, "what a coincidence."

"Dude, I ain't gonna room with you. There's no way!"

Corey frowned and shrugged, still standing in the hallway by the bathroom door. "Suit yourself. I guess you could go sleep in the lobby. They already told us that no one could change rooms."

"I'm going down there," Jimmy said in a huff. "I'm gonna get this straightened out right now. They can't make me share a room with you."

"Dude, calm down, would ya?" Corey wanted to laugh. Jimmy was kind of cute when he got all pissed. "Before you storm out of here, at least let me finish telling you what I was trying to say earlier."

"I already told you, I'm not interested in nothin' you got to say."

"You were totally right about what you said," Corey said, plowing ahead with his explanation in spite of Jimmy's objections. "I should not have let my friend Megan do that. I shouldn't have gone along with it. I should have told that Renee woman right away that none of that shit was true."

"Damn right!" Jimmy said, scowling. "But you didn't."

"So when I got in there and got my golden ticket, I spilled my guts. I told them the whole truth."

"Ain't this supposed to be a singing competition?" Jimmy asked. "Why does all this personal stuff matter, anyway? Why would you feel like it was okay for you to lie, make stuff up about yourself? Why pretend to be my friend?"

"I wasn't pretending, Jimmy." Corey sighed. He stepped over to the bed, and Jimmy backed away from him. As Corey sat there, Jimmy began pacing back and forth in the hallway. "Why don't you sit down," Corey suggested, "you're making me nervous."

"I don't care!" Jimmy shouted. "I don't give a flip if you're nervous."

At this point Corey couldn't contain himself any longer. He burst out laughing, covering his face with hands, and then he flopped back on the bed.

"What? What's so… oh, you make me so flippin' mad! What's so gol darn funny?"

Corey removed his hands from his face and rolled onto his side. He used one arm to prop up his head. "You are. You're really cute when you're mad. Do you ever actually swear, though? Do you ever say 'fuck'?"

"Well, it's not funny! And sure… sure, I swear. I swear all the dang time!" His face was beet red. He turned away from Corey and stepped toward the door. Suddenly he spun around, his hands on his hips. "Did you just say I was *cute*?"

Corey nodded, staring wide-eyed at the irate country boy. "Afraid so," he said. "You gonna beat me up now?"

Jimmy squinted, scowling. "I ought to. I ought to clean your clock."

Corey was still grinning. "For saying you're cute?"

"No! For what you did… back in Detroit. And for what you're doin' now, making fun of me."

Corey pushed himself up into a sitting position on the mattress. "Dude, I swear I'm not making fun of you. I don't mean to laugh, but if you could only see yourself. Your face is, like, fire-engine red."

"Well, ain't that what folks is supposed to look like when they're mad?"

Corey held his arms out and shrugged.

"Would you get some flippin' clothes on?" Jimmy said. "You're buck nekid."

"Sure," Corey said. "If it bothers you. I still say you're cute when you're mad, though."

"Stop sayin' that!" Jimmy said. "What is wrong with you, anyway? Guys don't tell guys they're cute."

"Some guys do," Corey said.

"Are you sayin' what I think you're saying?"

"What do you think I'm saying?"

"Never mind. I'll wait in the hall till you get dressed." He stepped to the door and grabbed hold of the handle.

"No, wait," Corey said, standing up. "I can get dressed in the bathroom. What did you think I was saying?"

"It don't matter. Just don't be callin' me cute."

"Okay. No problem. I'll never say you're cute again. Even though you are." He unzipped his suitcase and began throwing his clothes onto the bed. "And if you were asking if I was saying I'm gay, yes! That's exactly what I was saying."

"Oh," Jimmy said, staring at Corey intently.

"Are you?" Corey turned to him, looking him in the eye.

"That's none of your business." He folded his arms defiantly across his chest.

Corey turned back around, sorting out his clothes and smiling to himself.

JIMMY was locked inside the bathroom, leaning against the door. What were the odds he'd end up assigned to the same room as that kid from Michigan? As if it weren't bad enough that Corey had manipulated and used him back in Detroit, now here they were sharing the same room, and the guy was making fun of him.

Jimmy really wanted to stay mad at him. He had every right, but it didn't help that Corey was strutting around the room in his birthday suit. Jimmy's heart was pounding in his chest, but it was something other than anger he was feeling. And his heart wasn't the only thing that was pulsing. He had a wicked hard-on straining against the tight denim fabric of his jeans.

He didn't want to trust the guy, and he definitely wasn't ready to acknowledge that he liked him. But Jimmy couldn't deny that Corey had apologized—twice now—and he'd helped Jimmy back at the airport when he was about to be trampled. It was weird how he'd been so confident, coming right out and admitting he was gay.

Part of Jimmy wanted to go back and tell Corey the truth about himself. He wanted to be brave enough to just be honest about who he was. He wasn't sure if the guy was really trustworthy, though. It could be another trick. Corey could just be trying to get Jimmy to confess something personal about himself—like he had before—and then later use it against him.

It didn't matter. It wasn't like it was any of Corey's business who Jimmy was attracted to. There certainly was no possibility of a romance between them. They weren't even allowed to do anything like that. He'd read all the rules, and he wouldn't dream of breaking any of them. This was his once-in-a-lifetime chance, and he was not about to blow it just because his roommate was some hot-looking blond kid with gorgeous eyes, a smooth, well-defined chest, and a cute little bubble butt.

"I did not just say he had a cute butt," Jimmy whispered. He reached down and squeezed himself, massaging the obvious bulge between his legs.

"Screw this!" Jimmy said, a little too loudly. He stripped off his shirt and turned on the water in the shower. Peeling off the rest of his clothes, he then adjusted the water temperature. Cold! He needed to stop thinking thoughts like this and get his head back in the game. He had a competition to win, and he couldn't allow any distractions to interfere.

Ten minutes later, it was his turn to step out of the bathroom in the raw. He found a robe hanging next to the shower and wrapped it around himself.

"I see you found my robe," Corey said as he walked past.

"This is yours?" Jimmy said. "Sorry, I thought it was... ya know, from the hotel."

Corey laughed. "It is from the hotel. I'm just messin' with ya." Corey was now fully dressed and sprawled out on his bed. He had the television on.

"Oh," Jimmy said. He opened his big suitcase and began rummaging through it, pulling out some clothes. Stepping over to the far side of his bed away from Corey, Jimmy slipped on a pair of briefs. He was still wearing the robe, so he was confident he wouldn't be giving his roommate a show.

"Whooot whoo!" Corey whistled.

Quickly Jimmy spun around and glared at him. "That's not funny!" He felt his face turning red.

"Sorry, I couldn't resist," Corey said.

"Look," Jimmy sighed exasperatedly, "we're stuck with each other... I mean if it's true what you said about them not letting us change rooms. So we gotta figure out how to get along."

"I think we're getting along just fine," Corey said. "But you know what? You're right. I shouldn't whistle at you and say things to make you feel uncomfortable. You're probably not used to...."

"To what?" Jimmy asked when Corey didn't finish his sentence.

"Uh, well, to other guys whistling at you and saying you're cute."

"This ain't the time nor place," Jimmy said, nodding for emphasis. "We're not here for messin' around. We're here for a music competition."

"Okay, then," Corey said as he jumped up from the mattress. "Then I guess I should try singing to you...."

"No!" Jimmy protested.

Before Jimmy could say another word, Corey had picked up a hairbrush from the dresser and was wielding it like a microphone. He began to sing:

If I could turn back time
If I could find a way I'd take back those words that
hurt you and you'd stay

He started dancing around the room, all the while staring directly at Jimmy. As he sang, he gave Jimmy a pouty, apologetic look, and belted out the words of the Cher song while using one hand to clutch his chest. He held out his arm, palm up, and looked into Jimmy's eyes, fluttering his eyelashes flirtatiously.

In spite of himself and his desire to be pissed, Jimmy couldn't help but smile. Suddenly he had to give in. He burst into laughter as he shook his head.

Corey thrust the hairbrush into his hand, as Jimmy tried composing himself. He then opened his mouth and began to sing, same song but second verse. When he got to the chorus, they were singing in unison. Corey crawled over Jimmy's mattress and stood beside him, draping his arm around Jimmy's neck as they shared the mic.

"Our first duet," Corey said when they'd finished.

Jimmy was cracking up, but then grew more serious. He felt a little bit silly. He was still in his bathrobe, hair still wet, and was holding onto some hairbrush pretending it was a microphone.

"Does this mean you forgive me?" Corey said. "Puh-leez?"

"I'll think about it," Jimmy said. He took a step away from Corey, then turned and handed him back the brush.

"Good! Then let's go eat. I'm starving."

"Yeah, that's right. They'll be serving dinner soon… then we have a meeting."

"Well, hurry up… unless you wanna just go like that." Corey looked Jimmy up and down, assessing his current attire.

Jimmy laughed. "Nah, I think I better get dressed. I don't parade around nekid like some people."

It was Corey's turn to chuckle. "I love the way you express yourself. Some of the stuff you say is so funny."

Jimmy furrowed his brows and cocked his head slightly. *How else would you say it? Nekid's nekid. Right?*

A BUFFET was set up in the conference room, and as Corey walked in, he soaked up the enthusiastic energy of the four hundred young competitors. Twenty-six was the maximum age to compete on *America's Next Superstar*, and there were contestants as young as fifteen. Everyone seemed excited and happy, acting as if they were all best friends. While it was true they were all in the same situation—all passionate about doing their best in the competition—there was no denying that once the performances began, it would be every man (or woman) for themselves.

Jimmy was right behind him and leaned over to speak into Corey's ear. "This here is our competition," he said.

"Scary, isn't it?" Corey said.

"And kinda sad. There's gonna be a lot of disappointment. So many of us...."

"Of *them*," Corey corrected him. "Dude, you can't think like that. You gotta be sure of yourself and know you can make it. Just keep thinking about why you're here. Think of your brother."

Jimmy smiled at him and nodded. "You're right. We're gonna kick butt tomorrow."

"Hmm, well, you can kick butt if you want. I'm gonna kick *ass*."

Just then Corey noticed a flash of fluorescent green. It was his punk rocker friend's Mohawk. "Jeremy!" he shouted. "Dude, you made it."

The punk rocker stepped over, offering a high five. "Hey, man, you too."

"Wow, I didn't think I'd see you again. I lost track of you back in Detroit."

"Well, this is it, man," Jeremy said. "Are you guys in line?"

"Uh... not yet, I guess. Jeremy, this is my roommate Jimmy."

It took them nearly twenty minutes to make it through the buffet line, and then the three of them got a table toward the back of the room. When Corey spotted Sam, he motioned her over. She had another girl with her, perhaps her roommate.

"Hey, Teri," Jimmy said, offering a warm smile.

"You two know each other?" Corey asked.

"We met in the elevator," Teri said.

"How weird," Sam said. "You two know each other, and we know each other." She pointed to Corey. "And we're each other's roommates."

"And what am I?" Jeremy said. "Chopped liver?"

"I'm Sam and this is my roommate Teri," Sam said, providing an official introduction. "And you are *anything* but chopped liver." She winked at the studly rocker.

"It's gotta be the tattoos," Corey said sarcastically. "Sam, I can tell already you're a bad girl."

"Bad to the bone," she said.

The girls pulled out chairs and joined the table, placing their trays in front of them.

"You know Jimmy?" Corey asked. "He's my roommate."

"Howdy," Jimmy said, nodding obligingly.

"I saw you back at the airport when you about got trampled," Sam said. "You all right?"

Corey noticed Jimmy's face begin to flush. "Klutz, I guess," Jimmy acknowledged.

"And now you two are roommates," Sam said. "Small world, huh?"

"So you guys ready for tomorrow?" Jeremy asked. "Only half will make it."

The group let out a collective sigh. "And then it's on to group round," Teri said. "If we all make it through this first round, we should form a group together."

"That's not a bad idea," Jeremy said, "except you can't officially start rehearsing until all of the solo round has been completed. There's a room here in the hotel that has computers in it. They'll give each group an iPod and then you go to the computer database and pick out a song. There are thousands of songs in there. You just choose the one you want, print out the lyrics, and start rehearsing."

"How do you know all this?" Sam asked.

"I was a contestant two years ago," Jeremy said. "Made it through the solo round but got booted during groups. This time I wanna make sure I'm in a serious group."

"Well, we can start practicing even before the solo round is finished… unofficially," Corey suggested.

"Long as we don't put the cart before the horse," Jimmy said. "Gotta make it through the solo round first."

Corey laughed at the outdated metaphor. "True, but the solo round is three days. If we get lucky and make it through in the first or second day, that'll give us some lead time."

"But if one or more of us don't make it," Jeremy said, "that will change everything. We'll have to find replacements… or relearn our parts."

"It's just I've seen it on TV, right before group, there are always a bunch of people scrambling around trying to find a group to join," Teri said. "I don't wanna be one of those people."

"Well, this gives us a starting point, anyway," Corey said. "Once we have the solo competition behind us, we'll all know where to start looking…."

"No offense, dude, but we're all kinda different," Jeremy said. "Not sure I can even do country." He looked right at Jimmy.

"I'm flexible," Jimmy said. "I can sing about any kinda music."

"We were singing Cher together a few minutes ago," Corey said to back up Jimmy's statement.

"Cool… well, let's do it, then," Jeremy said.

"Do you guys mind if I sit here?" All eyes turned to the newcomer, a slender blond kid who Corey thought looked no older than twelve.

"Sure," Corey said, "more the merrier."

"Thanks," he said with a smile. "I'm Tristan."

"Dude, how old are you?" Jeremy asked. "You look, like, ten."

He laughed and looked down at his plate. "I *do* look young, I guess, but then so does Justin Bieber."

"You *do* look like Justin Bieber," Sam agreed. "Do you sing like him?"

"God, I hope not," Jeremy interjected.

"Actually, I like him," Tristan said, "and yeah, sometimes I sing his songs. That's what Krystal said during my audition, that I reminded her of Bieber."

"Well, it's nice to meet you, Tristan," Corey said. "This is Sam, Teri, Jimmy, and Jeremy."

"Where are you guys from?"

"Sam and I are from Michigan," Corey answered. "Jeremy's from Toledo, Ohio, and Jimmy's from Kentucky. I don't know where you're from, Teri."

"California," she said. "Los Angeles."

"I'm from Denver," Tristan said. "This is my first time in New York. First time anywhere, really."

"Ain't your folks with you?" Jimmy asked.

"Nope. My mom couldn't come. She takes care of my grandma, and she couldn't be gone for that long. Well, hopefully it'll be long… if I make it through the competition." Tristan's voice was quiet, and Corey thought he seemed shy.

"Well, don't worry," Jimmy said, "we'll look out for ya." He turned to Tristan and winked.

Corey didn't like the way the kid responded. It was like he was checking Jimmy out, maybe even flirting with him. Corey bit his lower lip and turned away, starting a conversation privately with Sam.

They were still eating when an official stepped up to the podium positioned at the front of the conference room. She was a twentysomething woman, wearing a pantsuit. She introduced herself as Margaret Billings, and she began by congratulating all the contestants. For the next forty-five minutes, she went through a presentation, covering the itinerary and explaining all of the rules, most of which were a repeat of the things Corey had already been told.

After she finished speaking, she turned over the program to a far more enthusiastic presenter named Harry. He had a wiry frame and a nasally voice, and his movements were very animated when he spoke. He explained the reality-show aspect of *Superstar*, reminding everyone that there would be a lot of cameras. "Try to act natural," he said. "Pretend the cameras aren't even there." He went on to explain that the film crews would be looking for interactions. After filming a particular scene, they might pull some of the contestants aside and interview them privately. He warned against speaking directly to the camera. "It'll come across as phony most of the time," he said. "If there are comments you want to make to the audience, save them for your private interviews."

When Harry finished his presentation, they were dismissed.

"Well, it was nice meetin' y'all," Jimmy said.

"Don't you wanna go do something?" Sam asked. "We're in New York, City," she reminded them, "and the night is young."

Jimmy shrugged. "I think I'm gonna stay here… go back to my room and practice for tomorrow."

"Me too," Tristan said. "If you want, you can come over to my room, and we'll practice together."

"What'd be the point?" Corey interrupted. "I mean, it's a solo competition."

"Oh, okay," Tristan said. "Sorry, I just thought…."

"It's okay, kid. If we make it through, we can practice together for group. I mean, if you wanna be in our group."

"Sure," he answered, his voice going up an octave.

"Well, good luck tomorrow," Jimmy said as he rose from his seat. "It was nice meeting everyone."

Corey glared at Tristan after Jimmy had left. The kid was being so obvious. He clearly had the hots for Jimmy and was flirting. He tried laughing it off, telling himself it didn't matter, but for some reason it bugged him.

"Guess I'll go back to my room too," the kid said.

"Good luck tomorrow," Teri said.

Once he was gone, Corey turned to Sam. "Didn't it seem like that kid was a little strange?"

"What do ya mean?" she asked. "He seemed okay to me."

"I don't know. I just kept thinking he was... ya know... flirting with Jimmy."

Sam cracked up. "Dude, the kid looks like he's in junior high. I don't think you have anything to worry about."

"I don't know what you're talking about," Corey said defensively. "Who said I'm worried? I was just making an observation."

"I think you're jealous," she said.

At this point, Jeremy and Teri were talking with each other, not listening to Corey and Sam's conversation. "That's crazy. Why would I be jealous?" Corey asked. "Jimmy doesn't even like me... and I couldn't care less what he thinks of that kid. Or of me, for that matter."

"Oh, okay. If you say so."

"Anyway, I'm gonna go back to my room," he said.

"Dude, no way!" Sam objected. "We gotta go do something. I didn't come all the way to New York just to sit in my hotel room."

"Well, if we make it through the solo competition, we can celebrate. But Jimmy's right. We need to focus on this first, or at least I do."

"Well, wait. At least give me your cell number before you go."

They exchanged numbers before Corey headed back to his room. In all honesty, he knew he didn't need any more practice. He'd rehearsed his song a thousand times. What he really needed was to get back to his room and check on Jimmy. He didn't like the way things had gone at dinner. There was no question that Tristan had been hitting on him, and Sam was right. It did make him a little jealous. Yeah, the kid looked really young, but he was cute, and Corey sensed that Jimmy had been attracted to him.

Well, Corey was gonna have to fix that. He needed to give Jimmy something else to think about.

WHEN Jimmy got back to his room, the first thing he did was call home. Charlie answered and was thrilled to hear his big brother's voice. Jimmy took a seat in the corner, using the only chair in the hotel room, and spent twenty minutes talking about his flight and the things he'd seen so far.

"And guess what? There's this kid here who looks almost exactly like you."

"Really?"

"Yeah, well, not exactly, but he reminds me of you. His name's Tristan."

"Is he… ya know, like you?"

"Oh, gay, you mean? Nah. Well, I don't know. I guess I didn't even think of that. I doubt it."

"That's cool, though," Charlie said. "It'll be like watching myself on TV."

"Yeah, they're gonna start the cameras tomorrow. Ya know who *is* gay, though? My roommate."

"Wow. Do you like him?"

"I dunno. I didn't like him at first. I met him back in Detroit when I auditioned. He was kind of a liar."

Charlie laughed. "How can you be 'kind of' a liar?"

"Let's just say he fibbed a little to get on the show. I didn't like it."

"Can he sing?"

"Oh, he can sing. His voice is amazing. Very talented."

"So he's your competition," Charlie reminded him.

"Well," Jimmy sighed, "I'm not really thinking of anyone in that way just yet. We're all here for the same reason—to get through this week. I'm tryin' to be friendly to everyone."

"Just remember, bro, if that dude would lie to get on the show, he'd probably do anything to win. So watch your back."

"Good point," he said. Just then the door opened and Corey walked in. "Hey, listen, I should get goin'. I gotta practice and get ready for tomorrow."

"Call me afterward," Charlie said.

"I will. Hey, I love ya, man."

"Love you too."

Jimmy set down his phone and looked up at Corey, who was now standing by his bed. "I thought you were goin' out with the gang," he said.

Corey shook his head and flopped down on his mattress. "Nah, you were right. I need to focus on tomorrow. It's too soon to go out celebrating."

"It's still early," Jimmy said. "Just 'cause I'm a homebody don't mean you gotta be."

"No, it's not that," Corey said.

"Well, I know we just ate, but I can get us a pizza later if you're hungry."

"Really?"

"Sure, why not?" Jimmy said. "Don't you like pizza?"

"I love pizza, but I've got to be careful. I don't have much money."

"I wouldn't have much either," Jimmy said, "but my daddy slipped me some cash before I took off. What kind of job you got up in Michigan?"

"I work at a grocery store. Cashier."

Jimmy grinned. "That's funny. I used to be a bag boy. Now I work at a garage."

"Really? You mean you're a mechanic?"

"Sort of. I work at one of those quick lube joints."

Corey raised his eyebrows and looked over at Jimmy, a smile on his face. "Quick lube, huh?"

Jimmy rolled his eyes and bent over to pick up his guitar. "You have a dirty mind," Jimmy said.

"What do ya mean? I didn't even say anything? I think you're the one with a dirty mind."

"So you're gay, huh?" Jimmy said. He didn't look at Corey when he said it. "You got a boyfriend?"

"Why?" Corey responded.

"Just wondered. Figured it was the polite thing to ask."

"Oh... well, no. I'm single."

There was a pause as Jimmy positioned the guitar on his knee.

"What about you?" Corey asked.

"What about me what?" Jimmy said, looking down at his guitar while positioning his fingers on the frets.

"Are you single?"

"Yeah," Jimmy said, then he strummed a note.

"Oh. I heard you on the phone, saying you loved someone."

Jimmy raised his head, unable to resist the urge to grin. "Yeah? Well, I get around. Don't mean I'm serious about any one person." He couldn't believe Corey thought he'd been talking to a boyfriend when it was only his brother.

"So does he think...?"

"What's it to you?" Jimmy asked. He strummed a couple chords.

Corey shrugged. "Nothin', I guess. I just...."

"I was talkin' to my baby brother, dude," Jimmy said, laughing. "I always tell him I love him before I hang up. Ya know, when you almost lose someone in your family...."

"Oh, sorry," Corey said. He lay back on the bed and covered his face with his hands as he sighed. "I just can't ever say the right thing to you," he complained.

Jimmy continued to stare at him. Corey looked kind of cute, the way he was lying there, stretched out. And there was no denying the guy had a nice body. Jimmy didn't respond to Corey's remark, but instead started strumming the guitar and singing.

It was a ballad, a Josh Turner song, one of Jimmy's favorites. The lyrics were quite suggestive. "Baby, lock the door and turn the lights down low...."

As he began to sing, Corey sat up again, looking over at him.

He got to the second verse: "There's no need to hurry, don't you worry, we can take our time...."

Corey pulled his legs up, sitting cross-legged on the bed as he leaned forward, listening to every word.

"Wow," Corey said, his voice a whisper. "That was... um... beautiful."

"You like?"

"Very much," Corey said. "The judges are gonna love your deep voice."

"Thanks," Jimmy said. "What's *your* song?"

"'Flying Without Wings'," Corey answered.

Jimmy immediately began to strum the guitar. He knew the song well, and as he played, Corey sang. The song began softly and built up to a crescendo, which Corey belted out. He was on his feet at the edge of the bed, hands outstretched, as he sang the words to Jimmy.

"Amazing," Jimmy said, setting the guitar on the bed beside him. Corey was out of breath and appeared on the verge of becoming emotional. "Are you okay, man?" Jimmy asked.

"It's the song." Corey reached up to wipe his eyes. "Maybe not the greatest choice. I mean... well, I don't wanna lose it tomorrow, get all emotional."

"You'll be fine," Jimmy assured him, "and even if you do cry, that's not always a bad thing. They might like it." He stood up and stepped over to Corey, placing his hand on his shoulder. "Trust me, they'll love it. You'll do great."

"Thanks," Corey said, smiling through his tears. "It's just... God, I'm so nervous."

"You think I'm not nervous too?" Jimmy said. "I'm scared out of my mind. If I get sent home during the first round, it'll be like everything I ever dreamed of has suddenly been shattered."

"I know," Corey said. "That's how I feel too. That's why...." He exhaled and looked into Jimmy's eyes. "That's why I picked that song. From the time I was old enough to walk, I've been singing. It's all I've ever wanted to do, but now here I am, grown up, working at a grocery store and going to community college."

"Least you ain't a grease monkey, like me." Jimmy winked at him.

"Someday you're gonna be a country megastar. Mark my words. It may be sooner than you think too. When I hear you sing, Jimmy, it touches my heart. You have one of the most beautiful, smooth voices I've ever heard. I don't think Josh Turner himself sings that song as well as you do."

In spite of all Jimmy's apprehension, when Corey said those words to him, he seemed sincere. Jimmy believed him. He reached up with his other hand and placed it on Corey's opposite shoulder, now holding him at arm's length.

"Thank you," Jimmy whispered. And then in spite of himself, he leaned in. It wasn't planned. It wasn't even logical, but it was the only thing he could do. He leaned in to press his mouth against Corey's. As their lips brushed together, they were startled by a banging on the door. Jimmy quickly let go of Corey's shoulders and jumped back.

Corey stared up at him, wide-eyed. "Uh, I'll get it," he said, spinning around and then stepping over to the door.

"Hi," Tristan said as Corey opened the door. "Sorry to bother you...."

"Come on in," Jimmy said. "We were just practicing."

"Are you sure it's okay?" Tristan said.

"Yeah, I'm totally sure. Come on, you can have pizza with us."

"Uh… I don't wanna intrude. It's just… uh, well, I don't have a roommate. They put me in a room by myself because one of my parents was supposed to come with me. My mom couldn't come, though."

"You're cool," Jimmy said. "Right, Corey?"

"Um, yeah, sure," Corey said, rather unconvincingly.

Tristan stepped in, and Corey closed the door behind him.

"Hey, I wanna show you something," Jimmy said. He reached in his back pocket and pulled out his wallet. "See this picture here? That there's my kid brother. His name's Charlie."

"Wow," Tristan said. He started laughing. "He looks… well, like *me.*"

"Weird, ain't it?" Jimmy said.

"Let me see," Corey said. "That's crazy. Same eyes, same nose." Corey took the wallet from Jimmy's hand and held the photo up next to Tristan's face. "Are you sure you two aren't related?"

"So do people tell your brother he looks like Justin Bieber too?"

Jimmy shook his head. "I don't think either of you look like Bieber. Maybe a little bit. You two look a lot more like each other. You're even the same height and everything."

"Your brother's hair is shorter," Corey said.

"In this picture it is," he said. "It's longer now. His eyes are a little different too. But anyway, there is definitely a resemblance."

"Maybe I'll get to meet him," Tristan said. "If we both make it through…."

"That'd be cool. Charlie's been sick, though. I don't know if he'll be up to traveling though. And if we make it through, we gotta go clear out to California."

Corey sat down on the bed and grabbed the TV remote from the nightstand. He turned the TV on. Tristan sat on Jimmy's bed, while Jimmy sat next to him in the chair. The three of them talked, and it became clear to Jimmy that Tristan was basically just a little nervous. He was a bit insecure and kind of freaked out being away from home by himself. He thought about Charlie's question on the phone, whether or not Tristan was gay, and Jimmy really didn't get the impression that he was.

Corey, on the other hand, didn't seem overly fond of Tristan. He noticed Corey rolling his eyes a couple times behind Tristan's back. At least he was being nice to the kid. Jimmy had already decided that he was going to look out for Tristan. As long as the kid was there, Jimmy would make sure he was all right. Maybe part of it was that he looked so much like Charlie.

After surfing through the channels a few times, Corey finally settled on a reality TV show.

"And now here we are on a reality show ourselves!" Tristan said. "It's gonna be weird tomorrow with all those cameras."

"They say that after a while you stop noticing them," Corey said. "Well, that's what contestants from *Real World* have said, like in interviews and stuff."

"On *Superstar* last year there was this one mother who was badmouthing all the other contestants," Tristan said. "She was saying all kinds of mean things about everyone and then going on camera to brag about how great her daughter was. Then when the other contestants were around, she was, like, hugging on them and being all nice."

"I remember that," Jimmy said. "She was a total B.I.T.C.H."

"You can say 'bitch', Jimmy," Corey teased. "Yeah, and then her daughter was one of the first ones voted off."

"So the moral of the story is: don't talk smack about people behind their back—at least not on camera," Jimmy summarized.

Jimmy was beginning to feel a little bit embarrassed. His thoughts kept returning to what had happened between Corey and him. He wondered where that kiss would have led them had Tristan not interrupted. A part of him wanted to get rid of the kid so that he and Corey could be alone again. Another part was thankful that Tristan had arrived when he had. He knew that the decent thing to do would be to invite Tristan to stay with them. The kid was obviously uneasy about being alone in his room, but Jimmy wanted some privacy with Corey.

Around eight o'clock they ordered a pizza and found a movie on TV. Corey had changed into comfortable clothes—a pair of sleep pants and a T-shirt, so Jimmy decided to do the same. He pulled out an oversized tee and a pair of shorts from his suitcase, then went in the bathroom and changed. When he came out of the bathroom, Tristan was sprawled out on his bed, lying on his belly with his head at the foot of the bed, watching the movie. Corey was on his own bed, sitting upright with pillows propped behind his head.

Corey stared up at Jimmy, a look of exasperation on his face. Jimmy smiled and winked, and then Corey quickly slid over, patting the mattress with his palm. Jimmy plopped down beside him, easing his back against the pillows. He looked over to Tristan to see he was engrossed in the movie, then glanced at Corey, who smiled sweetly. Jimmy didn't pull away when Corey slid his hand onto Jimmy's thigh. As they sat there watching the movie together, Corey began to rub his leg gently. When it became obvious that Tristan was starting to doze off, Jimmy stretched his arms out, wrapping one behind Corey's shoulder and pulling him against himself.

When the movie ended, Jimmy got up and grabbed a blanket from the closet, draping it over Tristan. He turned off the TV and dimmed the lights, then crawled back onto the bed next to Corey. "Good night," he whispered as he leaned in and gently kissed Corey's soft lips, then rolled over on his side, away from the boy he wanted so badly.

As he began to doze off, he tried to not think about the guy in bed beside him, but when Corey sidled up to him, spooning behind him, his heart began to race. Corey wrapped his arm around Jimmy's torso and then leaned in, whispering in his ear, "Thank you, Jimmy Sawyer. You're a really good kisser."

And they slept.

FIVE

THE more of Jimmy that Corey saw, the more he liked him. When Jimmy had sung to him the night before, it hadn't felt like Jimmy was just practicing for the competition. Corey felt that Jimmy was singing directly to him, and his heart had swelled. The rich, sensual tone of Jimmy's deep voice had moved him, and it felt like his heart had literally melted.

Jimmy must have felt it too. As Corey sang to him, Jimmy responded to his emotion. He responded in a way that was beyond anything Corey could have hoped for. That sweet, tender kiss had swept Corey right off his feet. Later, lying in bed with him, Corey had inhaled Jimmy's clean, masculine scent. He was so sexy. So incredibly manly, with his broad shoulders and hard muscles. Jimmy had a body that wasn't bulked up by weightlifting and steroids, but that was still tight and toned. Everything about him was straight out of Corey's wet dreams.

The way Jimmy walked, confidently with a firm, masculine stride, was enough alone to make Corey's heart skip a beat. Add to that the deep baritone voice, the dark-brown eyes, the sexy smile—Jimmy was sex on legs.

It didn't matter to Corey that Jimmy was nothing like the other gay guys he'd met. Clearly he knew nothing about fashion. He wasn't gossipy. Didn't swish and sashay and tell snarky, campy jokes. Jimmy was the kind of guy who probably had never said an unkind word about anyone. It was like he looked for the good in others, assumed they were trustworthy.

Perhaps that was naïve. Maybe Jimmy really was a hick who'd just fallen off the turnip truck, but Corey viewed him differently. Jimmy trusted other people because he himself was trustworthy. He was kind to other people because he was genuinely a good person, not because he was trying to manipulate others for his own personal gain. The way Jimmy had responded to Tristan was a case in point. Corey's gut reaction was just to get rid of the kid. He was annoying and immature, but Jimmy had treated him with such patience and understanding. He'd even gotten up and covered the boy with a blanket and had sacrificed his own bed.

Not that Corey was complaining. He hadn't minded in the least sharing his bed with Jimmy. It was a little embarrassing when he awakened the next morning hard as a rock. He hoped Jimmy had not noticed his arousal. Corey climbed out of bed and stumbled to the bathroom. After his shower, he discovered the two other guys were awake.

"Sorry I fell asleep," Tristan said. "I didn't mean to take Jimmy's bed. Jimmy, why didn't you wake me up? I could've gone back to my room."

Jimmy laughed and shrugged. "You were out like a light. Thought I should just let you sleep."

"Well, I better go back to my room now. I need to grab a shower before breakfast."

"Good luck today, kid," Jimmy said with a wink.

"Thanks, you too." He then turned to Corey. "And you too, Corey. Thanks again."

"Come back after your shower. We'll all go to breakfast together."

"Really?" Tristan said. "Okay, cool. See you in a few."

When Corey and Jimmy were at last alone in their room, the awkward silence was deafening. Corey was at a loss for words. He knew he should say something about what had happened, but he didn't know what. It wasn't a problem for long, because Jimmy hopped into the shower before Corey actually marshaled the courage to speak.

When Jimmy stepped out of the bathroom, Corey at last mustered the courage to open his mouth. "So I guess that answers my question?"

"Your question?" Jimmy repeated. He was rubbing his head vigorously with a towel.

"When I asked if you were gay."

The grin on Jimmy's face was priceless. Sort of a half smile, or smirk, and his hair was mussed... and he was wearing just a towel. Corey wanted to drop to his knees right then and there.

"I guess it wasn't such a good idea," Jimmy said.

"What wasn't?"

"What I did...."

"You mean kissing me? That wasn't a good idea?"

"Yeah. Against the rules 'n all."

"There is nothing in the rules about kissing," Corey insisted. "Just sex."

"And I don't even know I can trust you. I mean, after what happened...."

"I swear, Jimmy, you can trust me. And I'm not about to go broadcasting we're gay. I'm not here to come out of the closet to the whole world. I came to sing and to win a competition."

"I like you," Jimmy said. "You're cute and sexy and funny. You're really talented too, and I liked that you put up with Tristan last night. Most people would've just tried to get rid of him."

"I wanted to. I thought at first he was hitting on you."

Jimmy burst out laughing. "Dude, be serious."

"I *am*. I don't know how you can't see that he's majorly crushing on you."

"Well, I kinda have that effect on guys, ya know." Jimmy's voice was dripping with sarcasm.

"You really do."

"Tristan is scared. Alone in the big city, he's homesick. If it were my kid brother in that situation, I'd be thankful if someone befriended him and looked out for him. That's all I'm doing."

"So why'd you kiss me? After your speech yesterday… you know, when you said this wasn't the time or place."

"'Cause I'm a darn fool," Jimmy said. "'Cause there was this sexy, gorgeous guy standing right in front of me, and I… I just didn't think. I just did it."

"And then we slept together." Corey laughed.

Still grinning, Jimmy shook his head. "I gotta get ready."

Corey crossed the room and grabbed hold of Jimmy's face with both hands. He pressed his lips firmly against Jimmy's, this time not a gentle little peck. Jimmy chased his kiss, pulling Corey into him. Their mouths opened, and their tongues met, as Jimmy guided Corey backward toward the bed. The next thing Corey knew, he was flat on his back with Jimmy atop him, and they were kissing passionately.

Suddenly Jimmy pulled away.

"I'm sorry," he sputtered. "I've gotta get ready." He jumped up and grabbed the clothes he'd laid out on his bed, then rushed back into the bathroom, where he slammed the door behind him.

"We'll talk more later," Corey whispered.

THE auditorium where they began the competition was next to the hotel. The doors did not open until the celebrity judges arrived in their limousines, which meant that all four hundred contestants were waiting outside. The camera crews were also there, filming conversations and conducting interviews.

Jimmy carried his guitar case on his back as he followed Corey and Tristan into the crowd. When they spotted the fluorescent green Mohawk, they knew they'd found their friends. Jeremy had his arm around Teri, and Sam stood by, an unenthusiastic look on her face.

"You okay?" Corey asked her.

"Uh, could you ask me that again, a little quieter?"

"Sam got a little carried away celebrating last night," Teri explained.

Sam's voice was hoarse, and Jimmy couldn't believe she'd do something like that right before the competition. "Sam, are you gonna be able to sing?"

"Oh, I'll sing," she said. "I just need a little more water. Hopefully I don't have to perform early this morning."

A few people around the edge of the crowd began to cheer, indicating they'd spotted the judges. One of the crew members stepped up and motioned for the crowd to separate, parting them like the Red Sea to create a path for the judges to enter the building. He then called someone on his cell phone, and seconds later the doors to the auditorium opened.

Reuben was the first to get out of his limo. Wearing sunglasses and a stone-faced expression, he walked briskly toward the door. He stopped for a moment when he got to Jimmy and his friends. "Good luck," he said soberly, and then he continued inside.

"Who was he talking to?" Corey asked.

"I dunno. All of us, I guess," Jimmy responded.

As soon as the judge was inside the building, the doors were pulled shut.

"I guess none of us get to go in until all the judges are here," Tristan said.

"Photo ops," Jeremy explained. "They'll take footage of each judge arriving and then splice them together, make it look the Oscars. The judges arriving in limos and walking down the red carpet."

Jimmy looked down, and sure enough, the runner leading to the front of the door was bright red. It was another fifteen minutes until the next judge arrived—Krystal. Tyler and Raymond followed closely behind. After all the judges were inside, the doors were opened for the contestants. As they entered, each of them was handed a program schedule.

"Wow," Corey said excitedly, "they have assigned everyone a time."

"It's tentative," Jeremy said. "They're not likely to stick to it exactly, but at least it gives you an idea when you will be performing."

"I'm only the fifth name on this list!" Corey said.

"Dude, you're lucky," Teri said. "You'll have it over with quick."

"But… if I don't make it through…."

"You'll make it," Jimmy assured him. "At least the three of us are all on the Day One page." He was referring to himself, Corey, and Tristan.

"Oh, thank God," Sam said. "I'm not scheduled till tomorrow. Can I go back to bed now?"

"No!" the other four said in unison.

"My mama always said, 'If you're gonna dance, you gotta pay the piper.'"

They all laughed. "No offense to your mama, but that piper can kiss my ass," Sam groaned.

Teri and Sam were scheduled on the second day, and Jeremy was day three.

"I might get moved up to day two if they make it through the round quicker than expected. They try to get them done a day early if possible. Corey, you're gonna be in the first group. They'll call like the first ten people backstage and get you set up. The judges will do like two or three groups and then take a break."

"Oh my God, I'm so nervous," Corey said.

Jimmy reached up and rested his hand on his friend's shoulder. "You're gonna do great. Just sing like you did last night, and you'll be fine."

It was another twenty minutes before everyone was in the auditorium. Many of the contestants were still milling about and socializing when Margaret Billings stepped on the stage and addressed the crowd. "Everyone please take your seats," she said authoritatively. "I trust that everyone received a program schedule. We'll begin by having the first ten contestants come backstage. When we get to the fifth contestant on the list, the next group of ten will begin prepping. Be respectful of your fellow contestants. There is no talking or rehearsing allowed in the auditorium during performances. Each contestant will be given their results immediately following their performance. Those who do not make it through to the next round will have twenty-four hours to check out of the hotel. Those who do make it through are encouraged to remain in the auditorium and be supportive of the remaining contestants. Good luck to everyone. Without further ado, let's begin with the first ten performers."

Jimmy reached down and grabbed Corey's hand, squeezing it. "Good luck, man."

"Thanks," he said, and then he headed down the aisle toward the front of the auditorium.

"You like him, don't you," Tristan whispered into Jimmy's ear.

Jimmy turned to the shorter boy, smiling. "Sure, don't you?"

"Yeah… but not like that." The kid must've seen Jimmy holding Corey's hand. Jimmy didn't know exactly what to say. "It's cool," Tristan said, "I won't say anything to anyone."

"Thanks," Jimmy said, winking at him.

Ten minutes later, the first contestant was on stage. It was a girl named Brianna, and she was extremely nervous. Sadly, she botched her song, beginning in the wrong key and then forgetting some of the lyrics.

"That was painful," Reuben chastised her. "I've heard lounge singers that weren't half as bad."

The entire crowd groaned at his remarks, and Jimmy empathized with the poor girl. She must be mortified. Krystal was much nicer. "Sweetie, I'm sorry. You were just so nervous, but that's a part of entertainment. You have to be able to rise above your emotions."

Needless to say, she was voted off by unanimous decision.

The next two contestants fared much better, both making it through. Contestant four did okay, but he was a little pitchy. He didn't make it. At last it was time for Corey.

"Corey Dunham," Raymond said, as Corey stepped to center stage. "What'll you be singing today?"

"'Flying Without Wings'," Corey said confidently, and then he began to sing.

As he reached the climax of the song, he moved closer to the edge of the stage, stretching his arms wide and belting out the powerful lyrics. The crowd began to applaud as he hit his high note, and soon everyone was on their feet, giving him a standing ovation.

Even the judges stood, well, three of them, anyway. "Beautiful!" Krystal exclaimed. "Corey, that was absolutely amazing."

"Dude, you set the bar! You're in it to win it!" Raymond shouted.

Tyler leaned into his microphone, flipping his long hair to the side, "Man, that was incredible," he said in his raspy voice. "You definitely can sing."

Reuben sat there with his arms crossed. "Well," Krystal said to him, "give us your words of wisdom, oh mighty Reuben."

"It was okay," he said, "though a bit karaoke. Corey, if you want to be taken seriously in this competition, you're going to have to give a memorable performance. What I saw here today was nothing more than a rehashing of a 1980s boy band."

Krystal reached over and slapped Reuben on the shoulder. "Don't listen to him," she shouted into her mic. "Corey, you were magnificent!"

The crowd applauded and cheered.

"Let's vote," Krystal said. "I say yes."

"Yes."

"Hell yes!"

"Very well," Reuben conceded, "you're through to the next round."

"Thank you! Thank you so much!" Corey exclaimed, pumping his fist in the air before heading offstage.

"I MADE it through!" Corey shouted into his cell phone.

On the other end of the line, Megan squealed delightedly. "I knew you'd make it! Now what?"

"Now it's on to group competition, which will be Thursday."

"You got a group picked out yet?"

"Sort of. Remember that guy from Kentucky? Jimmy. The one who's brother was sick?"

"Uh, yeah, of course I remember." Corey wondered if it was a tinge of guilt he was hearing in her voice. "What about him?"

"Well, he's my roommate, and if he makes it through, we're gonna be in group together."

"Oh my God," she gasped. "Corey, be careful!"

"What do ya mean?"

"After what happened in Detroit, I wouldn't trust him."

Corey couldn't believe what he was hearing from his best friend. "Jimmy didn't do anything back in Detroit. If anyone should be leery, it should be him. We were the ones who knifed him in the back... and ya know what? I feel like shit about it. I'm just glad I had a chance to make it up to him."

"Hold on a minute," she said. "You didn't do anything to that kid, and neither did I. We just did what we had to do to get you an audition."

"I don't know. He got an audition and made it through, and he didn't have to lie about it."

"Let's not argue, okay? I'm just happy you made it through! All I'm asking is that you watch your back."

"Thanks," Corey said, "but I don't think I've got anything to worry about, not with Jimmy. He's a great guy, and he'd never betray me."

"Did you call your mom yet?"

"I'm doing that next. I just stepped outside to call you. Then I'm going back in to watch some more of the competition."

"Okay, baby. Good luck in group, and let me know. I can't wait to tell everyone you made it through the first round."

"Love you."

"Love ya too, sugar."

Corey ended the call and turned around, nearly crashing into Jimmy, who was suddenly standing behind him. "Oh," Corey said, "how long have you been standing here?"

"Long enough," he said. Jimmy reached out and placed his hand on Corey's arm. "That was a nice thing you said about me."

"Well, it was true."

"But you didn't tell her everything."

"You mean about us? About us kissing?"

Jimmy just smiled.

"Megan's got a big mouth. When I'm ready to tell the whole world about something, I just tell her. She doesn't need to know every detail of my life."

"Now you can relax," Jimmy said. "For a day or two, anyway. It's my turn to be nervous."

"Well, if they liked me, they're gonna love you," Corey said.

And Corey was absolutely right. The judges did love Jimmy, and even Reuben was kind in his remarks. Though Reuben had previously made no bones about the fact that he didn't particularly like country music, he couldn't deny that Jimmy's performance was spectacular.

It was when Tristan took the stage and began to sing that Corey held his breath. The kid definitely had a fantastic voice, but it was obvious he was extremely nervous. At one point during his performance, he faltered, and Corey feared it would be his demise.

Raymond immediately voted no. Tyler was undecided, and Krystal voted yes. The deciding vote went to Reuben. "Not the best song choice," he said, "but you have the stage presence and the voice. I vote yes."

The three of them had made it through! And it all happened on the first day. This was a cause for celebration. After sitting in the auditorium the entire day, the three boys left a bit early. They were all starving and took a cab to the Hard Rock Café.

It was after eight o'clock when they made it back to the hotel. Their spirits were high, and they were chattering nonstop, mostly about the competition, debating which song they'd choose for their group performance. As they walked into the lobby, Sam was at the front desk, and she had her suitcase.

"Sam, what's going on?" Corey rushed up to her.

"I got called to sing today after all. They made it through about thirty of the contestants on the Day Two list. I didn't make it through." Her voice cracked, and tears formed in her eyes.

"Oh no," Corey empathized, grabbing hold of her and hugging her tight. "Sam, I'm so sorry."

She pulled back and shrugged, tossing her head to the side and flipping her hair from her face. "I guess it's my own fault. I never really recovered from last night. I still don't completely have my voice back."

"It's not really fair," Corey complained. "All day long you weren't even planning on singing."

"I wasn't even there for most of the day," she said. "I happened to go back around four thirty and discovered they'd started calling from Day Two, so I had no choice but to hang around."

"Can't you stay here one more night?" Corey asked. "You've got twenty-four hours."

She shook her head. "I just wanna go. It's too hard... seeing everyone that made it. I'd just rain on your parade."

"Aw, no, you wouldn't."

"It's too late now anyway. I already got my ticket. My plane leaves in three hours. But listen, you've got my number, and you don't live that far from me. We'll have to get together. I know you're gonna go far in the competition, and I'll be rooting for you."

"Thanks," he said, feeling his own eyes well up with tears.

"And I'll vote for you too, once you make it to Hollywood."

"Do you know if Jeremy and Teri sang today?"

"No, Teri will be one of the first ones tomorrow morning, and I bet they'll get to Jeremy by the end of the day."

Sam's departure was sobering. It was a stark reminder of how quickly everything could change. Of course, she wasn't the only one that day to face defeat. More than half the contestants received the crushing news that their journeys had ended. Although Corey was ecstatic that he and Jimmy had made it through, he couldn't help but feel sad about Sam.

When they got back upstairs, Tristan headed back to his room. He said he was going to take a shower and maybe a nap. Corey was kind of relieved. At last he'd have some time alone with Jimmy. Corey flopped down on his mattress as soon as they entered their room, and he let out a huge sigh. He felt an odd combination of exhilaration and sadness.

"I can't believe Sam didn't make it," he said. "How disappointing."

"I know, but we knew it could happen. Overall, we're lucky. Both of us and Tristan all made it through...."

"You know every single one of us is in the same situation," Corey said. "Every contestant wants to win. For most of us, it's been a lifelong dream. The worst thing about Sam's case is that she got voted off on the first day. There've been all these weeks of anticipation after the auditions in Detroit."

"I know what you mean," Jimmy said. He sat down on the bed beside Corey. "I'd lie in bed at night and listen to my own heart pounding in my chest. Then I'd close my eyes and imagine what it would be like to be up on that stage performing for the whole world."

"And you know, we could be the next ones to go. Any one of us could be cut. In fact, most of us will be cut, and when I think about it that way, I'm scared shitless."

Jimmy placed his hand on Corey's chest. "No matter what, we're in this together," he said.

Corey stared directly into Jimmy's eyes and nodded. "I'm so glad it was Sam and not you," he whispered.

Jimmy leaned over him and they kissed.

SIX

REUBEN had just finished with a bath and was relaxing in his silk pajamas and robe when the phone rang. He set down his scotch and picked up the receiver. "Yes?" he said curtly.

"Mr. Jameson, there is a young man here to see you."

"Very well, send him up," Reuben said.

About four minutes later, he heard the knock on his door, walked over, and let in the boy he'd summoned.

"Hello, Tristan." Reuben smiled as he motioned for the boy to enter.

"Mr. Jameson, I got this note. It was delivered to my room, and it said you wanted to see me."

"Yes, yes indeed. Won't you come in? Can I offer you something to drink? A beer, perhaps?"

Tristan laughed nervously. "Is this a test or something? I'm not old enough to drink, and it's against the rules."

"Ah, well, I won't tell. And no, it's not a test. Sometimes rules are meant to be broken."

"It's okay, sir. I don't drink anyway. Maybe a soda or a water."

Reuben stepped over to the bar and opened the refrigerator. "Cola?"

"Sure, that'd be fine. Thank you."

Reuben led the boy into the living room area of his suite. "You're probably wondering what this is all about. Why don't you have a seat? Get comfortable. I just want to talk to you."

"Thank you, sir," he said again. Reuben could tell the boy was nervous. "I really appreciate you giving me another chance today. I know I screwed up a little bit."

Reuben laughed. "Indeed you did. It was quite horrendous, actually. You must've been quite surprised to make it through."

"Pleasantly surprised. Like I said, sir, I really appreciate it."

"Where are you from again, Tristan?"

"Denver," he said, sipping his cola.

"Ah, that's right. I remember now. I've thought about you quite a bit since that audition. You were quite impressive, and like I've always said, success in this industry is about memorable performances."

"Thank you," Tristan said, gulping.

"You have a decent voice, young man," Reuben went on, "but more than that, you are the whole package. You have the look. The perfect, cherubic face with the big blue eyes. You're angelic, and you're sure to be the next teen heartthrob."

He could see the boy's cheeks flushing. His embarrassment only added to his appeal, and Reuben sat down beside him on the sofa. "You've nothing to be embarrassed about," Reuben assured him. "I'm only speaking the truth." He reached over and placed his hand gently on the boy's shoulder.

"Thank you, sir." Tristan's voice was quiet, very meek.

"But if you're going to truly succeed in this business, you need someone to guide you. You need a mentor, someone to look out for you. There are a lot of vultures. A lot of people would be eager to take advantage of boy like you—so pure and innocent."

The boy slid away from him, inching his way down the leather sofa. "Uh, sir, I don't know what you mean."

Reuben was not dissuaded. He moved closer to the young blond, reaching up to run the back of his hand across Tristan's smooth cheeks. "Tristan, you want to win the competition, don't you?" he said.

"Uh, yes. Yes, sir, of course I do."

"I'd like that too… really, I would. But you know, sometimes winning involves more than talent."

"What do you mean?"

"I mean, it's not all about you. It's not just about you having a good voice. You have to win over the hearts and minds of the entire country. I can help you do that, Tristan. I can make sure you succeed."

"I appreciate it, sir. I really do…."

"Tristan, why don't you take off your shirt, get comfortable?"

"My shirt?"

"Yes, relax a little, and let me see your body. I want to see how smooth your chest is."

"Sir?"

"I want to touch you, make you feel good."

Tristan jumped up off the couch. "Mr. Jameson, I… uh… I'm not like that. I think you got the wrong idea about me…."

"Tristan, take off your shirt and sit back down." He patted the sofa cushion beside him. "I'm not going to hurt you. I swear. I'm your friend here, and if you cooperate with me, I can guarantee you that you will succeed. You *do* want to succeed, don't you? You don't want to go home just yet, not when you just got here?"

Tristan stared at him for a moment, not saying a word. Then slowly he reached down and began unbuttoning his shirt.

JIMMY had gone down to the lobby to get some refreshments from the vending machines. He purchased a couple Cokes from the soda dispensers and was headed back to the elevators when he happened to glance up and see a boy standing outside by the main entrance. It was Tristan. He decided to go over and check on him, see if he wanted to watch a movie again. Just as Jimmy made it to the automatic doors, a limousine pulled up. The driver got out and walked around to let Tristan inside.

That was weird. Where would Tristan be going in a limo? Maybe it wasn't Tristan after all. Maybe there was another kid at the hotel who looked like his brother. Maybe it was Justin Bieber. Jimmy laughed and shook his head. No big deal. He really wanted some time alone with Corey anyway.

When Jimmy got back to their room, Corey was lying on his bed. The television was on, but Corey didn't seem to be watching it. He was just lying there, staring up at the ceiling.

"Are you all right?" Jimmy asked, placing the cokes on dresser.

"I was just thinking," Corey said.

"About?"

"About how lucky I am."

Jimmy stepped over to his bedside and lowered himself onto the mattress. He placed his hand on Corey's arm. "You mean 'cause you made it this far in the competition?"

"Because even though I didn't have the easiest life growing up, I had a mom and a sister who loved me. Because I have friends who believe in me. Because the one single thing I'm good at and that I love with all my heart just might be the thing I'll be doing with my life.

"For a lot of people—most of them—that's all it ever is. Just a dream. A fantasy. What if I'd never gone to that audition? What if I'd told myself that the chances of winning were too slim, that I couldn't risk losing my job, that I was too scared to take a chance? That's probably what a lot of people do. They're too scared to step out on a limb.

"I know what Megan did to you wasn't right, but if she hadn't pushed me to go to that audition, I wouldn't be here. And if I hadn't gone to the audition, I'd have never met you."

"Well, I'm glad she pushed you," Jimmy said. "I'm real glad."

"How many people settle for a job and put their passion on the back burner?" Corey asked. "How many people know in their hearts they are destined to do one thing, but allow the events in their life to lead them away from that calling?"

"And that's what music is to you? Your passion? Your destiny?"

Corey pushed himself up to an upright position and leaned back against the headboard. "Yeah. It's more than just something I enjoy. It's my food. It's my water. It's the air I breathe. I can't describe it, but without music—without singing—I'm nothing."

"It's a kind of weird industry," Jimmy said. "So many of us—people like you and me—feel this way about our music, yet the number of people who succeed is so small."

"What if we don't make it, Jimmy? What if we get voted off before we ever make it into the Top Twenty-four? What then? Can you just go back to being a grease monkey at the quick lube? Can I go back to running a cash register?"

"For me it's about more than just being a star," Jimmy confessed. "Music is so much a part of my heart, that no matter what I do, it's always there. It's my salvation. It's my therapy. It's what I turn to when I'm happy or sad or scared. So, yeah, I can go back to being a grease monkey if I have to. No matter what happens in this competition, nothin's gonna take that away from me—my passion for music."

"When did you figure out…." Corey's words trailed off, and he left the sentence unfinished.

"That I didn't like girls?"

"Yeah."

"I played Little League, and when I was about twelve, I started noticing how cute the other boys were in their uniforms."

Corey laughed.

"Wasn't a big deal back then. Folks would tease me, say I was gonna be a lady killer when I got older. Said stuff like, 'You're gonna be a heartbreaker.' I just always expected that at a certain age I'd start to like girls. Then when all the guys I knew started talking about girls, sayin' stuff about their boobs and things like that... well, I didn't know what to think.

"I kept waiting for myself to change. I kept thinking that one day I'd just wake up and realize I liked girls. The day never came, though. Instead I started to see that it was guys that I liked."

"And it scared you?"

"Kinda," Jimmy admitted. "I thought it was a sin. I prayed about it. Then I met another boy who was like me. Keith was in my history class, and he lived just two blocks over from me. We started to hang out together, and I really liked him. I thought he was kinda cute too. He *was* cute. Big brown eyes. Really skinny. One day I couldn't help myself. I kissed him."

"Like you did to me?"

Jimmy smiled. "Almost exactly like that."

"What happened?"

"I dunno. I guess the same thing that usually happens. You meet someone in high school and fall in love. You think they're the love of your life and you'll be with them forever, but after a while, things change."

"So you broke up?"

"He was different than me. He started telling people about himself."

"He wanted to be out of the closet, and you weren't ready for that?"

"Yeah, I guess so...."

"But now?"

"After high school, everything is different. I finally told my brother, then my mama and my daddy. With Charlie being sick, it made me realize life was too short to live a lie. I didn't choose to be how I am. If I'm this way, it's 'cause the Good Lord made me, and if people don't like it, that's their problem."

"Jimmy, I never felt this way about anyone before—the way I do about you. You're the most wonderful guy I've ever known."

"You drive me crazy!" Jimmy said, suddenly standing up and pacing across the room.

"What'd I say?" Corey said, confused.

"Corey!" Jimmy said, exasperated. "You're all I can think about. Day and night. I can't get you out of my head. The things you say, the way you smile, even the way you walk. Last night when you curled up behind me in bed, I thought I was gonna just die!"

"And this drives you crazy?"

"You know the rules!"

"Fuck the rules!" Corey shouted.

Jimmy couldn't contain himself any longer. He lunged toward the bed, grabbing Corey by the waist and pulling him flat on his back. He then took the boy's head in his hands and kissed him passionately. "I want you so bad," he moaned.

"Jimmy, please...."

Jimmy continued to kiss him, driving his tongue into the boy's mouth, groping him, grasping at his clothing. Within seconds, their shirts were discarded, followed by their pants. They lay atop the mattress, caressing the smooth skin of each other's body. Jimmy felt Corey trail his fingertips up his back, then wrap his hands around Jimmy's shoulders. All the while he buried his face in Corey's neck, sucking and lapping his skin with his tongue.

Slowly Jimmy made his way down Corey's smooth body, finding his nipples. He took them in his mouth, one at a time. Corey cried out, bucking beneath him on the mattress as he grasped Jimmy's head, running his fingers through Jimmy's hair. Jimmy was so excited, his heart pounding, and his arousal raging in his boxers. He reached down to grab hold of Corey, and his anticipation increased exponentially as he realized the boy was equally aroused.

Unable to hold back a second longer, Jimmy peeled off Corey's shorts and took him into his mouth, savoring the hardness, the feel of that smooth skin against his tongue. He inhaled the musky scent as he devoured the young man he'd been obsessing over for the past twenty-four hours.

PART of it might have been the exhilaration Corey felt from making it through the first round of competition. It might also have been something as simple as hormones. Two young gay guys sharing a hotel room together, both attractive, both single. Those would have been the easy explanations.

But Jimmy was more to Corey than just a sexual outlet. He couldn't deny how attractive Jimmy was. Damn, he was hot as hell. With his tight-fitting jeans, deep voice, and confident swagger, Jimmy was the man of Corey's dreams. But even more importantly, Jimmy had a heart. He was a person of integrity. He loved his family, especially his little brother. He didn't tell mean jokes about other people, didn't laugh at someone else's expense. He was polite and kindhearted.

And it didn't hurt that Jimmy knew what he was doing sexually. When Jimmy went down on Corey, he thought he'd died and gone to heaven. The smooth, silkiness of Jimmy's warm mouth was unlike anything Corey had ever felt.

Of course Corey was eager to return the favor, and that part was even more exciting than being pleasured himself. Taking Jimmy inside of him, tasting him for the first time, was almost enough to make Corey come again. Corey had never known it was possible for a man to be both gentle and aggressive at the same time. Jimmy kissed passionately. He took control and was clearly in charge, yet the way he touched Corey made him feel as if he were being worshipped. He just seemed to know when to push and how far. When to lead and when to back off. When to dominate and when to make love.

All this after only one day. One beautiful night of lovemaking. Well, perhaps technically they hadn't made love yet, but even that didn't bother Corey. He was glad that there would be more to look forward to. He loved the progression—starting with a kiss, leading then to heavy petting, followed by pleasing each other orally. And then… eventually, if the time was right and they both were ready… they'd advance further.

Wasn't that how it was supposed to be? Wasn't it supposed to be about discovery and exploration? Wasn't it normal for his heart to swell and his pulse to quicken every time he thought about his boyfriend and what was in store for them?

The problem was that it all could end. Everything could be cut short in an instant. If either of them failed in the competition, they'd be ripped apart. Corey didn't want to think about that. He didn't want to contemplate that even if they were both extremely lucky and made it all the way through the first two weeks in New York, they'd be separated afterward. And then it'd be three months until they were together again.

It was a ten-hour drive from where Corey lived to Jimmy's hometown in Kentucky. After Corey got back home, he'd have to refocus on school and work. The semester had just started, and he'd have a lot of assignments to catch up on. He'd have to work as many hours as possible. The days he'd been gone would create a financial setback for him. Traveling to Kentucky was out of the question.

All he could do was make the best of the time he and Jimmy had together. He realized that they hadn't known each other long, not even two full days. But they shared a connection. Jimmy was the first person he'd ever met that had the exact same passion for his music. They related to each other on that level. Jimmy was the first person Corey had ever been comfortable enough with to bare his soul.

Corey sat at the desk in the hotel room later that night, writing an essay for his English class while Jimmy slept behind him. He'd made an arrangement with his professor, who was allowing Corey to document his experience at the competition in lieu of assignments listed in the syllabus. He'd have to turn in a term paper when he returned to class. His other instructors hadn't been as supportive but seemed to understand why he'd be absent for the two weeks. He'd miss their lectures, but was still responsible for the coursework.

"How long you been awake?" the groggy voice behind him asked.

"About an hour," Corey responded, turning in his chair. "You have bedhead."

"I know." Jimmy laughed. "If you still want me after seeing me in the morning—"

"More than ever," Corey interrupted. He got up from his chair and stepped over to the bed, offering a sweet wake-up kiss. "We can take a shower if you want," he suggested.

An hour later they were in the conference room having breakfast. Teri and Jeremy joined them, both nervous about the day ahead of them.

"I'm just freaked," Teri admitted. "After seeing Sam get cut, I'm scared."

When Jeremy grabbed her hand, Corey wondered exactly what was going on between them. A romance, perhaps? "Sam really fucked up," Jeremy said. "I really wasn't surprised she got cut. She didn't take it seriously."

"You know, she did, though. It's just that people deal with things differently. I think she was terrified of what might happen, and that's why she got so wasted the night before." Teri placed her other hand atop Jeremy's.

"Teri, you'll do great," Jimmy assured her. "And we'll be there to cheer you on. Then, as soon as you get it over with, we'll start rehearsing for group."

"I wonder where Tristan is," Corey said. He turned to Jimmy. "Did you text him?"

"He didn't answer," Jimmy replied. "I wonder if I should go up to his room and see if he's still sleeping. Maybe he decided to sleep in because he's done with first round."

"Yeah. Let him sleep. He'll probably see your text when he gets up and respond."

A few minutes later, they were all standing outside the theater, waiting for the judges to arrive. The crowd was much smaller than it had been the day before. Many of the contestants had been cut, and even those who hadn't were not necessarily motivated to show up to watch the remaining performers.

"Look," Corey said, pointing back to the hotel entrance. "Is that Tristan?"

There was a limo parked in front of the doors, and a boy who looked exactly like Tristan was getting out.

"I thought I was seeing things last night. I saw him getting into that limo when I was downstairs buying soda."

"What the fuck?" Jeremy said. "How much do you know about him? Is he rich or something?"

"I don't know," Jimmy said. "I don't think so because he said his mom couldn't come with him 'cause she had to work."

"That's so weird that he'd leave the hotel at night and then return in the morning," Corey said, "and by limo."

Tristan was already inside the building, so Jimmy pulled out his phone and tried calling him. Apparently he didn't answer, because Jimmy left a voicemail. "Dude, was that you who was just coming back to the hotel by limo? Let me know what's goin' on, okay?"

"He must've left his phone in the room," Jimmy said.

"Or doesn't wanna talk to you," Teri suggested.

Just then another limousine pulled up, this time stopping in front of the theater. It was Reuben. As he got out and headed down the red carpet, he was smiling uncharacteristically. "Wow, he's in a good mood," Corey whispered.

Reuben didn't say a word to anyone but just stepped briskly into the auditorium, and the doors closed behind him. Shortly afterward, the other three judges arrived, and the contestants were let in. Teri was in the second slate of performers, and her performance went well. She made it through, and the three guys heaved a collective sigh of relief.

"That just leaves you," Jimmy said to Jeremy.

"I know," he said, nodding. "Thing is, Reuben hates me. He doesn't like my hair or my piercings. It's hard to impress him."

"But there are three other judges," Corey reminded him. "If you do well, they'll put you through no matter what Reuben says."

"In theory," Jeremy said, "but I think Reuben has a lot of influence."

"Don't worry, Jeremy. Even if that's true, there's nothing you can do to change it," Jimmy said. "All you can do is give your best performance and hope for the best."

"Plus it's all being recorded," Corey said. "How can he be prejudiced against you when the whole world is watching?"

"Well, they don't show all the performances during this part of the competition," Jeremy pointed out. "They'll splice tape together to show just a few of the contestants."

Three hours later, Jeremy got his chance. As he took the stage, Teri and the boys cheered wildly for him, and his song was phenomenal. Corey was sure that there was no way he wouldn't make it through... until Reuben opened his mouth.

"Every dog in America is howling at this moment," Reuben complained. "That was about the most horrendous thing I've ever heard."

Tyler quickly rushed to Jeremy's defense. "You nailed it, man. Dude, you were rockin' the house. I can't wait till you get some instruments behind you, an electric guitar...."

"Sweetie, give us a moment," Krystal said. "We need to discuss this." The four judges huddled together, but no one could hear what they were saying. Apparently their mics had been turned off. After about three minutes, Krystal returned to her microphone. "I'm sorry, baby, you didn't make it this year."

Teri gasped, and Jimmy reached down to grab hold of her hand. "Aw, I'm so sorry," he said sympathetically. She pulled away from him and headed straight for the aisle. Jeremy was hanging his head as he exited the stage. Corey watched as the two of them rushed to each other, embracing. Teri was crying openly.

"That sucks," Corey whispered. "He should have made it through."

"Maybe he was right about Reuben," Jimmy said. "Maybe he does have influence over the other judges."

"It's really weird. I would have thought if anyone would be cut, it'd be Tristan, but Reuben loved him."

THE mood was very somber at dinner that night. Jimmy had gone to Tristan's room to check on him, and found him sitting alone. It was odd, because he had the blinds pulled and wasn't even watching television. "Are you okay?"

"I have a migraine," Tristan explained. "It's starting to go away."

"I thought I saw you earlier… getting out of a limo."

"Oh?" Tristan said, forcing a grin. "Well, it must've been someone else. I've been here all day, sleeping… or trying to. I have my phone turned off."

"You want to join us for dinner?"

"Yeah, I'll get cleaned up and meet you down there."

So Teri was depressed because of what happened with Jeremy, and Tristan was quiet due to his headache. "Guys, we have to pick out a song and start practicing," Jimmy reminded them.

"They're done with round one, and that gives us a whole day to practice," Corey said. "Why don't we meet in the lobby tomorrow morning, and we can rehearse all day?"

"What are you guys doing tonight?" Jimmy asked.

"I'm staying in," Tristan said. "I still don't feel great."

"Homework," Teri said. "If I don't keep up with my classes, I'll be screwed. After what I saw today, I'm not gonna count on making it through this competition. I think I'd better stick with Plan A: a college education."

"Teri, you can't let yourself get defeated. You made it through! We're all sad about what happened to Jeremy, but do you think he'd want you to give up?"

"You're right," Teri said. "It just sucks. But I really do have to work on this paper. I haven't done any homework since I got here."

"I did a bunch this morning," Corey said, "but you're right. I should do the same thing myself."

So Jimmy and Corey had a quiet night together in their room. They used Corey's laptop to watch music videos, debating which ones they liked and which ones they could possibly choose for the competition.

"Tristan's acting weird," Jimmy said. "He's depressed or something."

"Dude, migraines are a bitch. My mom gets those sometime, and they kick her ass. He's just lucky he got his when he did. If it'd been a day earlier, he might not have been able to perform."

"Do you think I should go check on him?" Jimmy asked.

"Why don't you call him? If he's up to talking, he'll answer. If not, you'll know he wants to be left alone."

When Jimmy tried to call, he again got Tristan's voicemail. "It's weird how he was so afraid of staying alone in his room, but now that's all he wants to do," Jimmy said. "I think something's wrong. Something more than a migraine."

EVERYONE was in a much better mood the following morning. The group spent the first three hours rehearsing their song and then met with a voice coach and an accompanist in the afternoon. Several times during their practice sessions, the camera crews came around and filmed them. Each of the group members was pulled aside for private interviews and asked really generic questions. "How's your group rehearsal going? Is there any one in your group you're not getting along with? Who would you say is the leader of your group?"

Corey realized the purpose of the interviews was to try to create drama. Since the four of them were getting along well together and they were making significant progress, they didn't get as much attention as some of the other groups. At one point another contestant, a girl named Shannon, came to them and asked if she could be in their group.

"We've already learned our parts," Teri said, "and we'd have to change everything if we added a fifth person."

"But Shannon needs a group," Jimmy argued. "We can't just leave her to fend for herself."

"Let's vote on it," Teri said. "That's fair, isn't it?"

Jimmy sighed. "Okay, well, I vote yes."

He looked at Corey, who immediately felt uncomfortable. He agreed with Teri. It would be a pain to change everything at this point. Shannon had had the same amount of time as the rest of them to find a group. It was her own fault if she waited so long. But Corey didn't want to disappoint Jimmy.

"Okay," Corey said. "I vote to let her in."

"No," Tristan said. "It's not fair."

"So it's a tie," Teri said.

"I can't believe you, Tristan. What if it were you that couldn't find a group? What if we hadn't let you join ours?" Corey said. He was instantly pissed. When Tristan was alone and looking for friends, Jimmy had invited him to join the group, now he turned around and defied Jimmy.

"It's okay," Jimmy said. "Tristan has a right to his opinion. But we haven't solved anything."

Just then Shannon, who'd been standing a few feet away out of earshot, stepped over to interrupt them. "You guys, thanks anyway, but I found another group."

"Oh, good," Jimmy said. "I mean, it's good you found a group… I'm glad for you."

"No problem. Good luck, you guys."

"I don't like that chick," Teri said, after Shannon had left. "She's a whiny bitch, and that's why she got kicked out of her last group. She'd have ruined it for all of us!" Just as she finished her tirade, Corey looked up to see the cameraman filming their conversation.

Oh, great. They'll put this on the show for sure.

By eight o'clock that night, they'd rehearsed their song at least a hundred times. "You guys, I think we've got it," Jimmy said. "We all know our parts. The harmony is perfect. The solos are fantastic. I think we should call it a night."

"You guys wanna come up to our room? We're gonna order a pizza," Corey said.

"I can't," Tristan said.

"Okay," Jimmy said. "Not feeling well? Is it another migraine?"

"Just tired," he said.

Corey thought the whole thing was weird. Maybe Jimmy was right about Tristan. Something was going on with him. But then again, none of them really knew each other all that well. Maybe the kid was just moody. Maybe he had bipolar disorder or something.

Corey chatted with Teri while Jimmy pulled Tristan aside to talk to him. "So you gonna join us?" Corey asked her.

"Yeah, for a bit. I am kinda hungry."

They headed to the hotel lobby, where Corey got a take-out menu from the front desk. He called in a pizza order, and the threesome sat on the sofas waiting for it to arrive. "So what's goin' on with him?" Corey asked. "Did he tell you anything?"

"I don't know," Jimmy said. "He just says he's tired. Maybe homesick."

"Seems like he'd want to be around people if he was lonely and homesick, though," Teri said.

Jimmy just shrugged.

After the pizza arrived, they headed up to their room. "I love this crust," Teri said, as she bit into her first piece. "So what's goin' on with you two?"

"What do ya mean?" Corey said.

"Well… Sam told me about you. She said you were… ya know, gay."

"Yeah?"

"And what about Jimmy?"

"We're both gay," Jimmy said. "But nothing's going on. We're both just trying to do our best in the competition."

It kind of hurt Corey to hear Jimmy say it. It was true, they'd just met. They'd only been roommates for a couple days, but he felt that what they'd done together was a little more than "nothing going on." Corey bit his tongue and didn't respond.

An hour later, after Teri had said goodbye and headed back to her room, Corey confronted Jimmy. "Why'd you tell Teri there was nothing going on with us?"

"I dunno," he said innocently. "I'm sorry, but I thought you were the one who said you didn't want to come out to everyone."

"Yeah, but you *did* come out to her. You just denied being my…." Suddenly it dawned on him. How could he expect Jimmy to put a label on them? They weren't boyfriends. How could they be when they'd only met each other, like, three days ago? But he wanted it to be more. He wanted it to be so much more.

"Corey, I want it to be more. I really do. But how can we even think about that now? If one of us gets cut, we may never see each other again. And even if we do both make it through, it will be three months till we're together again in Hollywood. And then we'll have to keep everything a big secret."

"So what you're saying is that we can't have anything together? We just had sex with each other one time and kissed a few times… and then we're just supposed to leave here and forget we ever met?"

"I'm saying we have to stay focused on winning the competition. That's all we can think about now, and sort all the rest out later."

"You know, I don't even know if there'll be a later." Corey felt tears well in his eyes.

Jimmy stepped over to him and placed his hand on Corey's shoulder. Corey turned away.

"Just leave me alone. I'm tired and I wanna go to bed." He grabbed some clothes from the dresser drawer and stormed into the bathroom, locking himself in. He stood there, leaning against the door as hot tears streamed down his cheeks.

JIMMY lay in the dark, sleeping in his own bed for the first time. He wasn't really sleeping, though. He was staring at the wall, his back turned toward Corey. This should have been an exciting day for him. Here he was, in New York City, a contestant on *America's Next Superstar*, and he'd made it through the first round of the competition. He was in the Top Two Hundred, and no matter what happened from this point forward, no one could take that away from him.

Jimmy felt good about their chances tomorrow. The group was strong. They all knew their parts. They had the lyrics down, and they knew every note. But Jimmy wasn't feeling elated. The excitement he was supposed to be feeling had been eclipsed by two troubling realities.

The secret Tristan had confided in him was horrifying, and Jimmy didn't know what to do about it. There was a part of Jimmy—that visceral, protective side of him—that wanted to go track Reuben Jameson down and beat his face in. At the very least, he had to report it, but he didn't know to whom. And he'd sworn to Tristan that he'd keep the secret. He'd promised not to tell another living soul.

He knew Tristan was gone for the night. He couldn't even go find the boy and check on him to make sure he was all right. He was already over at the other hotel, in Reuben's suite, doing God only knew what.

Jimmy wondered how people like Reuben could get away with this sort of thing. Tristan was just a kid. Granted, he was seventeen, which was probably the age of consent, but he was so innocent. He was naïve and timid to begin with, so unsure of himself. Reuben had to realize that a boy like this was a prime target. He was powerless.

And to make matters worse, Jimmy had hurt the one person he cared about most. By denying his relationship with Corey to Teri, he'd made his roommate feel rejected. Of course Corey would feel as if Jimmy was ashamed of him. Why had he said such a stupid thing? Why had he answered the question at all? He should have just changed the subject, or better yet, told her it was not her business.

It was too early to know exactly where things would end up for Corey and him, but it seemed to Jimmy as if he'd completely blown it. He destroyed the chance they had. When he couldn't take it anymore, Jimmy finally rolled over, staring at Corey, who was curled in a ball, facing the opposite wall.

"Corey," he whispered. Corey didn't respond, didn't so much as stir. "I'm sorry for what I said. I didn't mean to hurt you, and I was wrong. I'll tell her the truth… I'll tell everyone if you want. The whole world. I really like you, and I don't want to lose you…."

Corey rolled over to face him. Though the room was dark, Jimmy could see the silhouette of Corey's face, a tear streaming down his cheek. Jimmy slipped out of his bed and dropped to his knees beside Corey.

"I'm sorry," Corey said, choking back a sob. "It's my fault. What were you supposed to say? Of course you couldn't tell her…."

"No, I should have thought about how it'd make you feel. I'm such a jerk-off sometimes."

"Jimmy…?"

"Yes?"

"Shut the fuck up and get in bed."

Jimmy scurried to his feet and slid under the covers beside his unofficial boyfriend. They wrapped their arms around each other as Jimmy's lips found Corey's.

"We'll figure it out," Jimmy promised. "No matter what happens in the contest, we'll find a way to make it work. We'll make *us* work."

"Promise?" Corey asked.

"I swear to God," Jimmy whispered before kissing him, more passionately than ever.

SEVEN

"WHERE the hell is Tristan?" Corey whispered. They were in the theater, sitting in the auditorium, and their group was scheduled to perform within the hour.

"I'll try calling him again," Jimmy said. He slipped out of his seat and headed down the aisle toward the lobby. Maybe he should go back to the hotel and check Tristan's room again, but he'd tried that twice already. The kid either wasn't in the room, or just wasn't answering the phone.

Just as Jimmy pressed the call button on his phone, the entrance doors opened, and Tristan stepped through. "Dude, where have you been?" Jimmy said. "I've been worried…."

"I'm sorry," Tristan said, out of breath. "Am I too late?"

"No, you're not too late, but what happened?"

Tristan stared at him, his eyes wide and teary, and shook his head. "Nothing. I can't talk about it."

"Are you okay?"

"Yeah, I'm fine."

Jimmy stepped over to him and placed a hand on his shoulder. "Hey, are you sure?" The boy looked into Jimmy's face and nodded. Jimmy pulled him into an embrace. "We've gotta talk about this. We gotta do something about that guy…."

"No," he whispered. "Jimmy, please. You promised. Let's just get through the performance."

"Can you even perform? Tristan, you're emotional…."

Jimmy felt the boy cling to him, pressing himself tightly against Jimmy's body as his own began to tremble. Tristan buried his face in Jimmy's shoulder and wept, his entire body shaking violently. Jimmy just clung to him, holding him as he cried.

"We need to cancel the performance," Jimmy said.

"No!" Tristan exclaimed. "Jimmy, you can't do that. We can't quit… it will ruin all of us."

Tristan was right. If they didn't sing, they'd be automatically eliminated, but how could they expect Tristan to perform in this state? "Come on," Jimmy said, "let's go to the bathroom. You need to wash up, and you can tell me what's going on." He led the boy down the hall to the washroom.

When they emerged ten minutes later, Jimmy had his arm around Tristan's shoulder. "Okay, we can do this," he said. "You know your part, and we're all ready."

"Thanks, Jimmy," he said.

As they stepped into the auditorium, Corey and Teri were turned in their seats, looking at them. They both hopped up and headed down the aisle to meet them. "Come on," Corey said, "they just called our group." The foursome then made its way down the aisle and headed backstage.

"Tristan, where were you?" Corey said in a stage whisper. He was obviously pissed.

"I'm sorry," he said. "I overslept."

"You overslept? *Today?*" Corey clearly couldn't believe the ridiculous excuse. He glared at Tristan, then looked over to Jimmy.

"It's okay," Jimmy said. "We're all here now. No matter what you're feeling, get over it. We can deal with all that afterward. Right now… sing!"

Corey nodded, as did Teri. What Jimmy was saying was true. The group had to stay focused. They couldn't allow their emotions to interfere with the performance. It was just too important. In group round, the pool of contestants would be whittled down again, this time by half. By the end of the day, only a hundred people would remain in the competition. Although the overall presentation by each group would factor into the judges' decisions, every individual singer would be judged. Before they left the stage, they would know their fate—if they had made it through or if they were being cut.

It seemed like only seconds later that they were ushered to their positions just offstage, behind the curtain. They were next. Jimmy peered out onto the stage where the previous group was standing. They'd just finished their song and the judges were rendering their decisions. Three of the four contestants did not make it. They were cut, and only one singer made it through.

Seeing it happen was very sobering. Jimmy knew his own group could face the same fate. They had to keep their head in the game. They had to deliver the performance that he knew they were capable of.

"Oh my gosh," he said, "we're next."

When the stage manager motioned them forward, Jimmy reached down to squeeze Corey's hand. "Break a leg," he whispered.

The song began with Teri. Her solo was the first verse, and as she belted out her lyrics, the other three sang backup. They joined her in the chorus, and then Tristan stepped forward to sing his part. Jimmy was next, followed by Corey. Of the four parts, Corey's was the most powerful, and he was the perfect candidate to deliver. As good as he'd been in rehearsal, it didn't compare to the way he sang on stage, with the music behind him, the perfect acoustics of the theater, and the atmosphere created by the professional lighting. As the four singers joined Corey in delivering the final chorus, Jimmy knew they had nailed it. They'd each mastered their parts perfectly, and at the last note, when the houselights came up, Jimmy was thrilled to look out into the audience and see the entire crowd on their feet applauding. They'd earned a standing ovation from their peers. Even three of the judges were standing.

Of course Reuben was the only judge who was unresponsive. He sat there, arms crossed, waiting for the applause to die down. "Very impressive," he said stoically. "Not the best song choice, but your delivery was above average."

"Dawg! You hit it out of the park!" Raymond shouted into his mic. "All four of you—spot *on*! You nailed every line. I didn't even hear any pitchiness. And, Teri, the way you led things off... Corey, the climactic moment... Jimmy, that deep baritone voice, and Tristan... what can I say? You were fantastic. You threw down the gauntlet! You're in it to win it!"

The other two judges were equally complimentary. It was Krystal who delivered the judges' verdict: "Guys, you're all through to the next round."

The four of them high-fived and hugged each other, jumping up and down ecstatically. Jimmy grabbed Tristan by the shoulders and looked right into his beaming face. "You did a great job, Tristan. I'm so proud of you."

If Corey heard him, he didn't appear to mind. Jimmy knew he should be showering Corey with such praise, but after what Tristan had been through the night before, it was a miracle the kid was even here to sing at all. Before leaving the stage, Jimmy turned to look at the judges. He made eye contact with Reuben, staring at him intently. After a couple seconds, Reuben looked away. Jimmy hated the man, and it was all he could do to hold himself back from storming off that stage and strangling him.

This wasn't a time for anger, though. It was a day of celebration. All four of the contestants rushed outside and immediately pulled out their cell phones to call home with their good news. They'd be going on in the competition. They all made it into the Top One Hundred and were at the halfway point. They just had two more solo performances to deliver, and God willing, they'd be in the Top Twenty-four with a ticket to Hollywood.

THE foursome spent their afternoon together, celebrating their victory, but they each were aware that their euphoria would be short-lived. That evening they'd be meeting with voice coaches, starting to prepare for their final performance before the last major elimination. The upcoming round would be far more formal than what they'd been through previously. They would go through all of the preparation any artist performing on television would normally endure. Hair. Makeup. Wardrobe. They'd have full musical accompaniment and a stage backdrop that was customized to their song. The one hundred remaining contestants would plan their performances this evening and then have only one day to rehearse.

So after a late lunch and some window-shopping, the group of four headed back to the hotel conference room. There were fifteen voice coaches, each assigned roughly seven contestants to advise. Corey discovered that his coach was none other than the notorious Stella Burbank. *America's Next Superstar* often ran segments where she was featured, and it was obvious that she was brutal and demanding. Corey held the handout in his hand and turned to Jimmy.

"Oh my God, I've got Stella," he moaned.

"She's supposed to be the best," Jimmy said. "You're lucky."

"I've seen her on TV, and she seems so mean...."

"Who you calling mean, boy?" Corey spun around to face the voice behind him. His mouth dropped open when he realized it was Stella herself.

"Uh... uh...."

"Well, I see my reputation precedes me," she said, laughing. "And which one of America's Next Superstars might you be, young man?"

Corey gulped nervously. "Eh, I'm Corey Dunham, ma'am. I'm... uh... sorry about what I said. I meant no disrespect."

"Don't ever apologize for speaking the truth. What you said was true. I am *supposed* to be mean. That's what they say about me, anyway, but that's because they don't know me. They don't know what it is that makes me tick.

"I believe my job is to create winners. Sometimes it's pretty damn easy. In fact, when you get to this stage of the game, most of the contestants I work with are very talented. It's not difficult to produce results when you have raw talent to work with. The challenge comes in because all these other coaches are also blessed with talented pupils. Baby, the competition is fierce.

"My job is to push you, to help you achieve your maximum potential. If some folks wanna call that 'mean', that's their business. In my opinion, I'm just doing my job."

Corey stared at her, afraid to speak for fear she was not quite done with her lecture. "Yes, ma'am," he squeaked.

"So, Mr. Corey Dunham, tell me about you. What makes Corey Dunham so damned special?"

Corey was about to open his mouth and tell Stella about how he'd always dreamed of being a singer, how he'd known from an early age that singing was his passion, but then he remembered the advice that Jeremy had given him back in Detroit. That was everyone's story. Every single person in the competition had the same dream and the same passion.

"I'm special because I'm destined to do more with my life than clean toilets or bag groceries in a supermarket. Nothing wrong with those jobs, but I've been blessed with an amazing talent, and I'm determined not to waste it! I'm special because I know that music is more to me than just a hobby. It's more than a passion. It's the center of my being. It's what I live for...."

Stella raised an eyebrow.

"And you are?" She turned to Jimmy.

"This is my *friend*, Jimmy. He's also a contestant."

"Is this boy telling me the truth?" She asked Jimmy. "Is he as special as he claims to be?"

Jimmy quickly shook his head. "No, ma'am. He's not as special as he says." Corey looked at him, puzzled. "He's far more special than that. He's got one of the most amazing voices I've ever heard, and he's a pretty great guy too...."

Corey didn't know what to say. He felt himself starting to choke up.

"Well, I'd say you're both pretty blessed. Jimmy, who's your coach?"

"You are, ma'am," Jimmy replied.

Corey had been so excited and nervous when he looked at his handout that he hadn't bothered to check to see which coach Jimmy had been assigned to.

"Well, now, ain't that convenient," Stella said. "Why don't you two come right over here, and we'll get started?"

"Now?" Corey said.

"Why not? We're all here...."

And so the boys followed her over to her corner, where she worked with each one of them. They spent a full two hours with her, first selecting their songs and then going through them, line by line.

"You know, Mr. Corey Dunham, I think you may have been right about how special you are. You're gonna do just fine. I'll be at rehearsals tomorrow, and I'll work with you some more then, but you're well on your way. I've worked with a lot of contestants over the years, and I've got a good track record for picking winners. I bet you a dime to a donut that the both of you make it to the Top Ten."

"Really?" Jimmy said.

She nodded emphatically. "Mark my words."

The boys each hugged and thanked her before they left, then headed back to their room. Corey was psyched. He felt a rush of adrenaline pump through his veins. How could any of this be real? How could it actually be happening to him? All his life he'd dreamed of *Superstar*, and now here it was... almost a reality.

As they entered the elevator and watched the door close them in together, Jimmy reached down to grab hold of Corey's hand. "Congratulations on making it through," he whispered. He then leaned over and kissed Corey on the lips.

"Thank you, sexy," Corey replied. "I love the song you picked out."

"I hope the judges do," Jimmy admitted.

"Oh, they will… well, three of them, anyway."

"Yeah, you got that right."

"What's up with that Reuben, anyway?" Corey asked.

"That man is a monster. He's an evil, evil man."

Corey laughed, staring up at Jimmy for a moment, then realized he was serious. "Jimmy, what do you mean? He's a jerk, but it's not like you to call people evil."

"Take my word. He's evil!"

"Okay, then…."

The door came open, and they headed down the hall toward their room, still holding hands. When they got to their room, Corey fished in his pocket for the key. After inserting it, he pushed the door open and looked down at the floor. There was an envelope bearing his name.

"Hmm," he said, scooping it up.

When he got inside, he flipped on a light switch and tore open the envelope. "Wow," he said, "speak of the devil. Reuben Jameson sent me this invitation. He wants me to meet him in his hotel room tonight… alone."

EIGHT

"YOU'RE not going!" Jimmy insisted.

"What do you mean, Jimmy? It's Reuben... Reuben Jameson. How can I say no to him?"

Jimmy snatched the letter from Corey's hand. "Let me see this."

"Jimmy, just 'cause he's an ass, and we don't like him doesn't mean I can just blow something like this off. If he wants to see me...."

"You don't understand," Jimmy said. He exhaled and walked across the room. After a moment, he fished out his phone from his pocket and made a call. "Dang it! Tristan must still be in rehearsal with his voice coach."

"Look, I have to get going. This letter says they're picking me up out front in, like, ten minutes."

"In a limo," Jimmy said.

"Well, yeah, in Reuben's.... Wait! Tristan came back that one day in a limo. Do you think...?"

"Yes, Corey," Jimmy said, frustrated. "Tristan has been going over to Reuben's hotel room every night."

"What? What're you talking about?"

Jimmy knew this was making no sense to Corey, and he was torn. He somehow had to convince Corey not to meet with Reuben, but he couldn't betray Tristan's confidence. He stepped over to Corey and grabbed him by the shoulders. "Listen to me," he pleaded. "You have to trust me. Don't go over there."

"Jimmy, calm down. Of course I have to go. Reuben's the head of the show. He's also a judge. If I ignore his request, I could get kicked off. And what's it gonna hurt? It just doesn't make any sense why he'd even want to see me in the first place...."

Jimmy looked Corey straight in the eye, not speaking.

"Oh my God," Corey said, a dawning of realization striking him. "Reuben is summoning male contestants to his room late at night. Then they're returning the next morning. And now... now he's picked me."

"Exactly! Corey, you can't go."

"But... Jimmy, I have to at least go over there. If he puts the moves on me, I can just tell him I'm not interested."

"And what're you gonna say if he tells you to either give him what he wants, or you'll be history?"

"Blackmail me? I know you think he's evil, but I doubt he's that bad...."

Jimmy nodded slowly. "Corey, he's that bad. Trust me."

"And you're telling me he's been doing this shit with Tristan already, all along? Dude, that's gross."

"I'm not telling you anything... or, well... I promised Tristan I would keep this secret. But I had to tell you—to protect you."

Corey stepped closer to him, pressing his body against Jimmy's chest. Jimmy wrapped his arms around the shorter boy. "Actually, you didn't tell me. I guessed. But what do I do?"

"We've got to report him," Jimmy said.

"What's there to report? And to whom?"

"I wish Tristan would call me back. I wanna get him to show you." Jimmy wanted to say more, but he couldn't.

"Jimmy, I know this much already. Just tell me. I won't let on that I know anything. Please...."

"All right," Jimmy sighed. He took Corey's hand and led him over to the bed. They sat on the edge of the mattress, and Jimmy turned to him before he spoke. "Tristan is really messed up," he whispered. "He has bruises and scrapes around his wrists where it looks like he's been tied up or handcuffed or something. He's got deep scrapes and cuts all across his back."

"What? From Reuben?"

"He's into bondage or something. He's beating Tristan, whipping him."

"No fucking way," Corey said incredulously.

"It started out that Reuben just wanted to touch him, fondle him. They had sex... well, Reuben's into all kinds of stuff. He does drugs. Tristan said he kept doing lines of coke and then... then after each line he'd want to have sex again. Every time more extreme."

"How?"

"He takes pills too. Drugs to keep him aroused."

"But, I mean, how is this happening? Why is Tristan letting it happen?"

"He's scared. Reuben told him point blank he'd be cut if he didn't cooperate."

"That's sick! And now... now he's picked *me*? Why me? Why Tristan?"

Jimmy slowly shook his head. "I don't know. I don't know how he chooses his victims."

COREY'S hand was shaking when he knocked on the door. He held his breath and waited, trying to hear if there was movement on the other side. After a moment the door opened. Reuben stood there, smiling wryly in his silk bathrobe. His welcoming expression quickly faded when he saw Jimmy.

"I thought I told you to come alone," Reuben said.

"We're together," Jimmy said.

"Well, you can just go back where you came from," Reuben said flippantly. "If I have need of you, I'll let you know... you'll have your turn."

"Look, we know what you're doing," Jimmy said as Corey stood there, looking on.

"I've no idea what you're talking about. On second thought, I have no use for either of you. You both may go." He began to close the door, but Jimmy pushed his way through. Corey followed him inside.

"I'm calling Security," Reuben said, stepping briskly across the room and picking up the receiver of the house phone.

"I wouldn't do that if I were you," Jimmy said.

"I don't know who you think you are...."

"Tristan Devere has bruises all over his body because of you."

"You've no idea what you're talking about...."

"He's fifteen," Corey exclaimed.

Reuben stopped, his mouth dropping open as he placed the receiver back in its cradle. "You're lying," he said. "I saw the paperwork. I saw his birth certificate."

"Don't you ever watch TV?" Jimmy said. "Sometimes a birth certificate is not enough. Did you ask to see the long form?"

Corey grinned. "Reuben, you've been fucking a fifteen-year-old kid."

"There is no proof," he said.

"You think these hotels don't have security cameras?" Jimmy said, stepping closer to him. "You think the bruises and lacerations all over that boy's body can't be photographed? Do you think Tristan didn't save the notes you sent over to him, summoning him to your room every night?"

Reuben reached up with one hand and wiped his brow, then stepped over to the bar, pouring himself a scotch. "What the fuck do you want?" he said. "What's your price?"

"Our *price?*" Jimmy said. "You're a sick bastard!" This was the very first time Corey had ever heard Jimmy swear. "We don't *want* anything from you. We want you to stop hurting our friend!"

"Mr. Jameson," Corey said, "it's right in the rules. Sexual contact is forbidden."

Reuben laughed. "So now you're going to lecture me on the rules… my *own* rules?"

"Okay, well, if you don't wanna follow your own rules, what about the laws of the state of New York?" Jimmy said. "I'm sure having sex with a minor—a fifteen-year-old boy—is not legal."

"You're bluffing," Reuben said. "The minimum age to be a contestant is sixteen, and Tristan Devere presented proof that he was of age at his audition."

Jimmy stood there, glaring into Reuben's face as the older man tossed back another shot. "The game is over, Reuben. Your child-molesting days are through…."

Corey could tell the man was scared.

Reuben stood there for a moment, obviously thinking. "You want an assurance? You want a guarantee that you won't be cut? I can make that happen. I can put you through to the final round… if that's what you want. I can make all your dreams come true."

"We do want an assurance," Jimmy said. "We want a guarantee that you'll stop hurting Tristan."

"Oh, for the love of God," Reuben said, pouring yet another drink. "The boy loved every second of it…."

Jimmy pulled out his phone. "I'm calling the police."

"All right! Wait, you have my guarantee. I won't touch him again."

"Or any of the other contestants," Corey said.

"Look," Reuben said, "I don't know who you think you're playing with here. I can make things really wonderful for you—for both of you. Or I can make your lives a living hell. I told you I won't touch your friend. Until you provide proof of the boy's age, that's all you're getting."

Corey looked at Jimmy, wondering what they should do. They had no proof of Tristan's age. Tristan was seventeen, and the whole thing really was a bluff, but they had at least gotten a confession out of Reuben.

"And if we get cut from the competition because our performance sucked… fine," Jimmy said. "But we better not be cut just because of revenge."

"You'll have your fair shot. If you're good enough to earn the votes of the other three judges, you'll go through, and I won't stop you."

"We don't want to hear from you again," Jimmy said, "unless it's when we're on stage." Jimmy reached in his pocket and pulled out a handheld recorder. "We'll see you at the next round." Then Jimmy turned and grabbed Corey by the arm, leading him to the door while Reuben was left standing behind them, mouth agape.

"What do you think is gonna happen?" Corey whispered after they were in the hall.

"He might try to kick us out. He might separate us…."

"But we have his confession on tape."

"Corey, once he finds out we were lying about Tristan's age, he's gonna be pissed. Hopefully the tape will be enough to save us, but there are always scandals associated with these shows. I'm sure he doesn't want the world to know he likes having sex with young male twinks, but he's an egomaniac."

"Let's go back to our room. This place gives me the creeps."

IT WAS 1:00 a.m., and the three boys were huddled together in Jimmy and Corey's room.

"Maybe we should call the media," Corey suggested. "The TV station or the newspaper. What about one of those magazines?"

"I think we need a lawyer," Jimmy said.

"No!" Tristan pleaded. "You guys, this would kill my mom if she found out. He said he'd stop, so let's just drop it."

"Tristan, we can't just drop this," Jimmy said. "Do you honestly think Reuben's gonna just drop it? He'll go after us, all three of us. He'll do anything he has to, to get rid of us."

Tristan's eyes welled with tears. "But you have the tape. He'll never risk it. He confessed on the tape. And we have the notes. We have witnesses...."

"That's why we need a lawyer," Jimmy said.

"But then my mom will find out."

"Your mom needs to know," Corey said, placing a hand on Tristan's shoulder. "Tristan, you are the victim here. You've nothing to be ashamed of."

"Tristan, if we don't stop Reuben, he's gonna keep doing this to other boys. He already said as much."

Tristan stood up and began pacing the room. "Why'd you have to go and interfere? He was probably done with me anyway. He didn't even call for me to go to his room tonight."

"Because he'd moved on to me," Corey said. "That's what he does. He uses people, and if I'd have submitted to him, he'd have just used me until he got tired of me and then moved on to his next victim."

"Look, I can't do this," Tristan whined. "I just can't. If you call the TV station or the police, I'll just deny everything."

"You can't deny it, Tristan!"

"This isn't my fault! Why are you doing this to me?"

Tristan was now sobbing. Jimmy stood up and tried to embrace him, lend him comfort, but the boy shoved him away.

"Please, if you care about me at all, you'll just drop it. Let it go away... I just want to forget it ever happened."

"Tristan... please."

"Promise me! You've got to promise you won't say anything to anyone. Reuben's not going to mess around with any other boys. He's too scared."

"Maybe for now," Corey said. "But he will eventually."

"Well, that's not my problem."

"Tristan, how can you say that?" Jimmy asked.

"Look, you're wrong about this whole thing. I'm not a victim. I liked it! Reuben was right. I loved every fucking minute of it, and I'm old enough to decide for myself. If they ask me anything about it, I'll tell them that. I'll tell them I begged for it, and you'll look like a fool."

"Tristan, I know you don't mean that," Jimmy said.

"I *do* mean it! Just fucking drop it!" Tristan stormed over to the door and rushed out of the room, slamming the door behind him.

"Now what?" Corey said, staring at Jimmy, whose jaw had unhinged.

Jimmy shook his head. "There's nothing we can do… other than sit and wait for the axe to fall."

nine

WHAT should have been Corey's dream come true had suddenly turned into a nightmare. He'd made it through the first two rounds of the competition and was fully prepared for the next round. He had a fantastic voice coach and had selected a song that was perfect for him. He'd met the most wonderful guy in the world and was crazy about him.

But now it all could be taken away. Corey was certain that Reuben would find a way to get rid of both him and Jimmy. He wasn't the kind of guy who liked to take no for an answer, and when he found out that Tristan was not really underage, he would surely retaliate.

What Tristan had said was disturbing. He'd claimed that he'd enjoyed it, that he was not a victim at all but rather a willing participant in Reuben's sexcapades. That statement made no sense. He'd gone to Jimmy looking for help. He'd already stated that Reuben was forcing him to do things he didn't want to do. It had to be that Tristan was just scared. He was embarrassed and afraid of what people would say. He was terrified his family would find out about what he'd done.

That was how people like Reuben got away with this sort of behavior. Nobody was brave enough to tell on him. And even if they did come forward, the allegations would be hard to prove. Sure, there were security cameras in the hotel, but without a court order, they'd never have access to them. And there were the notes that Reuben had sent, but they didn't prove anything either. The only evidence that they really had was the tape recording of their conversation with Reuben. But what he'd said on tape was that Tristan had loved every minute of it, and now Tristan was backing up that story.

Even if the boys found someone in the media to listen to their story, it would just turn into another one of those "alleged sex scandals." There were at least a couple of them every season, and no one really believed them. In the process of this revelation, they'd just end up hurting Tristan even more.

So Corey feared his days were numbered in the competition. Reuben would influence the other judges to vote him off the very same way he'd done to Jeremy. And Jimmy would go down with him. Corey wished now that he'd not shown Jimmy the note. He wished he'd have just met with Reuben secretly. Of course, that wouldn't have been possible. Jimmy was in the room when he found the note, and he'd have had no way of sneaking out.

All they could do now was give their best performance and pray that was enough. Corey lay in bed, cradled in the arms of his boyfriend. Yes, he was beginning to think of Jimmy as more than just a guy he liked. He knew that what they had was more than just a casual affair, and in fact, he could not imagine how horrible it was going to be saying goodbye when the elimination round was over.

"Jimmy," he whispered, not even sure if he was still awake, "I love you."

Jimmy's arms tightened around him. "It's gonna be okay," he responded. "Try not to worry."

It might have been a little easier for Corey to heed Jimmy's advice, if only Jimmy had returned his sentiment.

THE following day was all about rehearsal. Corey was thankful that the schedule was so busy. He met with the makeup artists, the wardrobe specialists, the hair stylist, the stage manager, his accompanist, and of course Stella, his voice coach. Both Jimmy and Teri had similar schedules, and the three of them saw far less of each other than they were used to. It seemed as if Tristan were nowhere to be found. Corey didn't run into him even once during the day.

Around four that afternoon, Corey had his first ever dress rehearsal on the *Superstar* stage. It was an exhilarating experience to be up there under the lights, dressed to the nines, belting out his song. He realized that this could be the closest he would ever get to being on the real *ANS* stage—the one in Hollywood where the whole world would be watching.

A half hour after Corey's rehearsal, Jimmy was scheduled, so Corey hung around in the auditorium. He took a seat and waited, and while he waited he texted his friend Megan. He told her about just finishing his rehearsal and how awesome it was. Before he knew it, it was Jimmy's turn. Corey put away his phone and sat there in the dark, watching.

When Jimmy stepped out on the stage, Corey caught his breath. The young man looked spectacular. He was wearing a western shirt and form-fitting jeans, and, of course, a cowboy hat. The way he walked across the stage so confidently, with that Southern swagger, was a thrilling sight. Jimmy was so damned sexy. Corey could just about lose control simply by looking at him.

It was the voice that really did it, though. Jimmy's baritone nearly sent Corey over the edge. Needless to say, his performance was flawless, and when he completed his song, Corey stood and applauded. Jimmy squinted, trying to see who was in the audience clapping.

Just then, Corey heard another pair of hands clapping behind him. He turned and saw that they belonged to none other than Krystal, one of the official judges. "Wow, isn't he amazing?"

Corey turned all the way around and smiled at her. "Yes. He's fantastic."

"He's sure to make it through," she said.

"Really?" Corey said. "How can you be so certain?"

"Well, assuming he performs like that tomorrow. You too, young man... Corey, isn't it?"

"Yes, ma'am," he said. "Thank you. Did you also see my rehearsal?"

"I did, and I'm very impressed."

"Krystal?" Corey said, hesitating.

"What is it, sweetie?"

"Can I ask you something?" He wasn't sure how exactly to ask her what he needed to know.

"Anything," she said, still smiling.

"If there is one judge who wants to get rid of a contestant, how much sway does he have over the other judges?"

She laughed and reached out to place her hand on Corey's shoulder. "Which judge is it that you're worried about, baby? Reuben?"

Slowly Corey nodded.

"Don't you worry about Reuben. His bark is worse than his bite, and to be honest, he really likes you. He likes both of you." She pointed to the stage at Jimmy.

"I'm not so sure. Not anymore, I mean."

"Why? What happened?"

Corey reached in the pocket of his suit jacket and pulled out a folded note. "Last night when I got back to my room, I found this note." He handed it to Krystal. "I was afraid to go by myself, so I took my roommate with me—Jimmy. Well, Reuben wasn't too happy...."

Krystal read the note with a puzzled look on her face. "I don't get it. Why would Reuben...." Her voice trailed off.

"We didn't do anything with him. I swear."

"Corey, have you shown this to anyone else?"

Corey looked down toward the ground, unsure of how to answer.

"Please, Corey, I have to know...."

"There's another boy, but I can't say who he is. He's been meeting Reuben in his room every night since we got here."

She folded up the note and handed it back to Corey. "Hold onto that, and guard it with your life," she whispered. "Listen to me, Corey.

Don't worry about Reuben. I'll make sure you and Jimmy get a fair shot in the competition. Just concentrate on delivering your performances, because if you screw up, there's no way I can save you. You know that Reuben has a lot of sway. He's the one who first started this show. He thinks of it as his baby, and sometimes he acts like he has more power than he really does."

"Well, what's going to happen? Are we gonna have to worry about him retaliating against us? What if he does? It's not like I can do anything about it. I can't even go to the media…."

She shook her head. "Don't go to the media. Like I said, just focus on your own performance, and I'll make sure Reuben doesn't hurt you."

"Thank you," Corey said.

"I've got to go now. Good luck tomorrow." She stepped closer to Corey, holding out her arms to hug him. "You just hang in there. I know you'll do great."

BOTH Corey and Jimmy gave flawless performances the next day, but they had to wait for their results. During this round of elimination, the contestants were not immediately given feedback. When Corey took the stage, he tried not to look at Reuben, and he had no idea what impression any of the judges had of his presentation. When he was finished, he took a seat in the auditorium and waited for Jimmy.

It was a long day, one of the most grueling of Corey's life. Sitting there waiting and worrying was horrendous. He hated the fact that the judges waited until all the contestants had sung before rendering their decision. After Jimmy's song, the two sat together. All they could do was wait.

After the last performance of the day, at seven o'clock that evening, the judges posted their results. The one hundred contestants were divided into five groups of twenty, and each group was sent to wait in a separate room. Two of the groups would make it through to the Top Forty, the other three groups would go home.

Corey and Jimmy did not end up in the same group.

"Crap!" Corey whispered.

"It'll be okay," Jimmy said. "There are two groups that will make it. Hopefully they're our groups."

Tristan and Teri ended up in a group together, but it was not the same group as Jimmy or Corey. This meant that at least one member of their foursome would be cut, possibly two. If Corey's and Jimmy's groups made it through, then Teri and Tristan would not. If Teri and Tristan were saved, then either Jimmy or Corey would have to go. Worst-case scenario would be that all three of their groups were cut.

Corey and Jimmy hugged before heading to their rooms. He knew that when they saw each other again they'd either be ecstatically happy or terribly disappointed. It was a horrifying feeling. As Corey sat in the corner, anxiously awaiting his fate, he prayed that Jimmy would make it. If Jimmy were cut, it'd be awful. Corey actually was more concerned about Jimmy than he was about himself. He knew that Jimmy would be able to go on without him, but he wasn't sure if the reverse was true.

Although it was less than an hour wait, it seemed an eternity. The four judges went to each of the rooms, delivering their verdict. The members of Corey's group looked at one another when they heard shouting and cheering coming from one of the other rooms. Apparently the judges had already delivered their results to that room, and it sounded favorable. Corey prayed that the shouting they heard was coming from Jimmy's group.

At last the door opened, and the judges stepped into their room. All the contestants were seated on the floor, looking up at the judges expectantly. It was Krystal who spoke.

"Well, first of all, I want to tell all of you that you should all be very proud. To have made it this far—into the Top One Hundred—is an accomplishment in and of itself. Unfortunately, we have the unpleasant task of choosing only forty people from this sea of amazing talent. The worst part of our job is delivering our verdict when it's time to make these very difficult cuts.

"So I'm going to just put you out of your misery and tell you... you made it through! You're in the Top Forty!"

The entire room erupted in uproarious cheers. The contestants were on their feet, pumping their fists in the air, hugging one another, many of them crying tears of joy. One of Corey's fellow contestants grabbed him and pulled him into a tight bear hug, even though Corey barely knew him.

"Please come downstairs to the conference room, where you can meet the other half of the *America's Next Superstar* Top Forty."

Everyone began racing out of the room, and as Corey stepped into the hallway, he immediately saw Tristan. He was standing with his arm around Teri, and they both were crying. Tristan looked at Corey and shook his head. They hadn't made it. Corey stepped over to them. "I'm so sorry," he said.

"Hey," Teri said, "this isn't the time for you to be sorry. You should be celebrating! You're in the Top Forty."

"I know, but I'm sad. I'm gonna miss you guys so much...."

"Corey," Tristan said, as he stepped closer, "thanks for everything. I knew you'd make it."

"Tristan, are you gonna be okay?" There were tears streaming down the young boy's cheeks.

Tristan nodded. "I am now. To be honest, I'm glad it's over."

Corey grabbed hold of him and hugged him tightly. He then embraced Teri. "We have to stay in touch," Corey said. "We have to promise each other...."

"Corey, go on and win," Teri said. "You deserve it. We should be the ones worried about you forgetting us after you're rich and famous."

They all hugged one more time, and then Corey pulled away. "I have to go. I'm supposed to go downstairs, and I don't even know yet if Jimmy made it."

Teri just smiled at him.

"You know something?"

"Just go," she said.

Corey smiled. Jimmy must have been in the other group that made it through, but his friends did not want to spoil the surprise. "I love you guys!" Corey said as he turned and dashed down the hall. He couldn't wait for the elevator, so he took the stairs, three at a time.

When he dashed into the conference room, he began scanning the crowd—the much smaller group of only forty. At last he saw the cowboy hat. "Jimmy!" he shouted.

Jimmy turned and raced toward him. "Oh my gosh! I thought you didn't make it! All these people came in, and you weren't here…."

Corey jumped into his arms, squeezing him tightly. "We made it! We both made it!"

"WE'VE only got one more round," Jimmy whispered, nuzzling his face against Corey's cheek.

"They've got to cut sixteen people," Corey said. "What if we've made it this far only to be eliminated in the final round?"

"You can't think that way. It ain't gonna happen," Jimmy said. He slid his hand down the center of Corey's back, resting it finally against his bottom. Jimmy liked the feel of the smooth, tight-fitting fabric of Corey's dress slacks. "You looked so sexy up there when you were singing."

"Oh really?" Corey said. His voice was soft and breathy, as if he were gasping for air. "I was sexy then, but not now?"

"Even more now," Jimmy said. He reached up and loosened Corey's tie, pulling it off, then proceeded to undo the top two buttons of his shirt.

"Sing that song for me," Corey pleaded. "That one you sang our first night."

"'Your Man'?"

"Yes… please."

Jimmy continued unbuttoning the shirt, leaning in to plant sweet kisses on Corey's pouty lips between each button.

"Baby, lock the door and turn the lights down low…," he crooned.

"Mmm… your voice. Your sexy, deep voice."

Jimmy only sang the first couple lines of the lyrics. His mouth was soon too busy with other tasks. Very gradually he inched his way down Corey's smooth chest, concentrating first on his right nipple, then the left. Corey whimpered as Jimmy grazed the sensitive nubs with his teeth. By the time the last button was free, Jimmy was on his knees, at eye level with Corey's waist, and it seemed only logical he shift his attention to the business at hand.

As he unfastened Corey's belt and unzipped his fly, Corey steadied himself by grabbing hold of Jimmy's shoulders. First the pants slid down Corey's thighs, followed quickly by his boxer briefs. Jimmy's pulse quickened as he savored the sight and smell of Corey's hardness. Unable to restrain himself any longer, he dove for it, devouring it in one ravenous gulp. As his mouth surrounded the pulsing hard-on, Jimmy moaned, enjoying the smoothness of the skin and the musky smell that wafted into his nostrils.

"Oh, God," Corey cried, trembling slightly.

Jimmy began to suck, slowly bobbing up and down, laving Corey's manhood with his tongue. Corey only allowed him to continue for a few strokes and then pulled out. "Jimmy, please… you'll make me come."

Jimmy grinned devilishly and looked up at him. "Ain't that the idea?"

"I want… Jimmy, I want you to make love to me."

Jimmy remained there in his kneeling position for a few seconds, looking directly into Corey's eyes. "Baby, are you sure?"

"I'm ready," Corey said. "I don't want to wait any longer."

Jimmy pushed himself up so he was standing directly in front of his lover. "Corey," he whispered, "I love you too," and then he pulled him into his embrace, delivering the most passionate kiss of his life.

And they made love.

Ten

IT WAS the last day of the elimination rounds. All of the performances had been given, the judges had made their decisions, and now the remaining forty contestants had to wait for the results. They gathered in the auditorium by the hotel and waited for their names to be called. One by one they were summoned to a back office where the judges would render their decision.

Out of forty contestants, only twelve males and twelve females would make it through. Jimmy surmised that the odds were not in his favor. He'd known from the beginning that he was not Reuben's favorite. He knew the competition was fierce. Although he hated to lose, mainly because he didn't want to disappoint his brother Charlie, he was ready to go home.

He'd be going home one way or the other after the results. If he made it through, he'd have to travel to Hollywood in three months to compete in the nationwide contest. If not, it'd be over, and he would at least be able to be proud of how far he'd gotten.

Over the previous three days, the contestants each had to give one final performance before the judges. It was extremely formal, and they all had spent hours rehearsing. Jimmy's song had been well-received. The judges seemed to love it—most of them anyway.

But Jimmy suspected that at this stage of the competition it was not really about the talent of the contestants. It was not about any one performance. It was about putting together a group of twenty-four performers who would blend together in a way that created an entertaining reality show. It was about balance. They'd select a variety of musical styles. They'd stack the top twenty-four with a balanced racial and ethnic mix. They'd try to represent several different regions of the country.

Jimmy was the only remaining male contestant that predominantly sang country western. He was the only contestant from Kentucky. Those were his positives. But on the other hand, he was in an age group that was overrepresented. There were three Southern opponents that also had thick accents. He was not a shoe-in by any means.

Corey, on the other hand, had a better shot. He was undeniably a heartthrob. He had that adorable, cherubic face. He sang beautiful love songs and ballads, and was a great dancer. He had a broad market appeal, and there really wasn't any other contestant remaining in the competition that was likely to rival him. Corey was also the only contestant remaining from the Great Lakes region. Jimmy had a lot more hope for Corey than he did for himself.

And if Corey went on without him, Jimmy would not be bitter. He'd be thrilled for his boyfriend. Yes, he considered Corey his boyfriend now, and he couldn't even imagine how painful it was going to be to say goodbye to him tomorrow. That night, three days ago, when they made love for the first time, had been a milestone for both of them. They'd embarked upon new territory, and each of them had shared with the other a part of himself that had previously been reserved.

Jimmy felt no remorse. He'd saved himself for the right person, and he knew that Corey was that special someone. Corey was the one who fulfilled him. Corey was the one who made his heart swell, who made him wonder how he'd ever lived prior to meeting him. And no matter what happened in the competition, Corey was Jimmy's superstar.

As they sat there in the auditorium, Jimmy glanced around to make sure no cameras were nearby, then reached down to take hold of his boyfriend's hand. Leaning over, he whispered in Corey's ear, "I love you so much."

Corey squeezed his hand and turned to face him, his eyes brimming with tears. "God, Jimmy, what the fuck am I gonna do without you? I can't go for three months without you! I love you so much."

"Corey Dunham!" They heard Corey's name announced, and Jimmy released his hand. Corey's was the first name called.

"This is it," Corey said. "Wish me luck."

"Break a leg," Jimmy said.

As Corey exited the auditorium, Jimmy could do nothing but sit there and wait. "Please God, let him get through." It seemed like forever as the seconds ticked by. Jimmy kept his head bowed, not daring to look up. Finally, ten minutes later, the doors at the front of the auditorium swung open, and Corey raced through.

"I made it!" he shouted. The remaining contestants rose and applauded.

Jimmy rushed over and hugged him, squeezing him so tightly that he literally lifted him off the ground. Corey squealed excitedly. "Oh my God, Jimmy. I made it! I really made it!"

Jimmy wanted more than anything to kiss him. Tears of joy streamed down both their faces. "You better call your mom," Jimmy said. "She's gonna be so proud."

"You'll be next," Corey assured him. "If I made it, you will for sure."

Jimmy smiled at him sweetly. "It's okay, even if I don't, I'm so happy for you."

"You *will*," Corey insisted.

They waited until the next contestant was called back, and then the two of them stepped outside so that Corey could have some privacy. He called his mother and told her the exciting news, then Megan.

"I better get back in," Jimmy said, "in case they call me next."

They didn't end up calling Jimmy right away, though. For the next two hours he sat there, waiting as the judges made their way through the forty contestants. He witnessed a lot of elated faces walk through the door and several contestants that were heartbroken. Regardless of what the outcome was, there were tears—either tears of joy or disappointment.

Jimmy was trying to count the number of male contestants who'd made it through. He knew there were at least six. That left only four slots, and there were seven other male contestants who'd not yet been called. It was just before four o'clock when he got called.

He stood up, and Corey grabbed hold of him, hugging him tightly. "I love you," he whispered. Jimmy looked up to see a camera in his face. He smiled sheepishly, though unashamed of the affection and support Corey offered.

"I love you too," he whispered.

As Jimmy walked through the door, he stepped into a long hallway. They must have reconstructed the stage area in order to create a corridor through which the contestants had to enter and exit. He imagined it was to add to the drama while they were filming. Whatever their reasoning, Jimmy felt like a dead man walking as he made his way down the long hallway.

At the end of the hall, he had to go through a doorway. It was a large oak door, and as Jimmy tentatively pushed it open, the first thing he saw was Krystal's smiling face.

"Jimmy Sawyer," she said cheerfully, "come on in and have a seat."

Jimmy stepped over to the chair and sat down. All of a sudden he felt like a teenager who'd been called to the principal's office. He smiled at Krystal and then glanced at each of the other three judges.

Reuben had a smug look on his face, and Jimmy could only imagine what he was thinking. In all honesty, he didn't care what that jerk thought of him. Even being in the same room with the man was almost more than Jimmy could stand. But it was Reuben who began the conversation.

"Jimmy," he said, clearing his throat. "Unfortunately, we are down to the very end, and we have to make some very important and often difficult decisions. Only the best of the best are chosen as our Top Twenty-four, and it is our responsibility to ensure that the American public is afforded the opportunity to vote for those who are truly the best.

"In my opinion, you are not one of those chosen few. In fact, I don't think you even come close to the caliber of talent that we are looking for—"

"But we all do not share Reuben's opinion," Tyler interrupted. The long-haired rocker leaned over and looked Reuben in the eye. "Some of us can appreciate talent when we hear it."

"And thankfully we operate as a democracy," Krystal said. "Reuben has his opinion, but he is only one vote. Jimmy, I was impressed with you from the moment I heard your audition. You have not once stumbled. You've delivered time and again, the most spectacular performances—songs that have given me goose pimples and have brought tears to my eyes."

"Jimmy," Raymond began, "Dawg, you got it! There is absolutely no question, you are in it to win it!"

"Jimmy," Tyler said, "by majority vote, you are in our Top Twenty-four!"

All of the anxiety and fear that had laid on Jimmy's chest suddenly was lifted, and with it rose a swell of intense emotion. Tears instantly came to his eyes, and he covered his face with both hands, rocking back and forth in his chair.

"Thank you! Oh, thank you so much!" he said, half as a prayer and half to the judges.

Three of the judges were on their feet, and Jimmy stood to meet them, embracing each of them one at a time. He turned to Reuben, thinking he should at least shake his hand, but the man was gone. He'd walked off the set.

The other judges didn't seem to care. They continued to congratulate him and slap him on the back. He ran down the hallway, which this time seemed much shorter, and burst through the door. "I made it!" he screamed, and instantly Corey was in his arms.

ELEVEN

"I LOVE him, and I can't wait until January to see him!" Corey protested. "I'm sorry if you don't like it, but I'm going."

"Corey, please," his mother pleaded. "You're going to California in January, and God knows how long you'll be gone. That's only a month and a half away. Why do you want to spend all this money on a trip to Kentucky now?"

Corey released an exasperated sigh. "It's only a week. I got the time off work, and I'll only be missing one day of classes. With the Thanksgiving holiday, there would be no classes after Tuesday."

"You realize this will be the very first Thanksgiving that our family hasn't been together."

"That's not true," Corey said. "Dad hasn't been with us for Thanksgiving since I was four. I'm spending Thanksgiving with Jimmy, but I'll be home for Christmas, and Jimmy's gonna be here for New Year's."

"Corey, honey, don't you think you might be rushing things a bit with this boy? You've only known him...."

"For almost two months."

"But you only spent two weeks together in New York."

"And have talked every single day since, sometimes a dozen times or more per day. Mom, do you wanna tell me what this is really about?" He pulled out a kitchen chair and sat down at the table.

"I've told you—"

"No, you've told me a list of excuses, but there's something more."

"Corey," she said, tossing her dishrag into the sink and then turning around to face him, "I'd hoped you'd outgrow some of these notions. I just expected... well...."

"You expected me to meet the right girl and put all this crazy gay stuff behind me? I'd fall head over heels and be swept off my feet, and I'd forget all about the fact that I like boys instead of girls?"

"Corey, you're going to be a celebrity now. I don't think you even realize the implications. Your face is going to be on every television set in the country... maybe the world. You'll have no privacy, and neither will our family. Do you really want this homosexuality issue to come out?"

"Mom, I'm gay. That'd be like asking a black contestant if he wanted his race to come out...."

"You're being ridiculous," she said, placing her hands on her hips and shaking her head, infuriated.

"Look, I already did meet the person of my dreams. I already was swept off my feet. It's just this person happens to be a boy rather than a girl. I'm sorry if you don't like it, but I hope you'll be able to get over it somehow, because Jimmy is going to be in my life a long, long time. I love him! I *love* him!"

Tears were streaming down his mother's cheeks. "I should have known. I should have sensed it... well, actually I did. I knew you were different when you were young. Even before you started school. The signs were all there, but I thought you'd outgrow them."

"Mom, what are you talking about?" Corey pushed his chair back and stood up, stepping toward her.

"I might have been able to get you some help... cure you."

At this point it was Corey whose eyes filled with tears. "Mom," he gasped, "I'm not sick. I don't need a cure." He turned and stormed out of the kitchen and out of the house.

WHEN Corey stepped off the plane in Lexington, his heart was racing with anticipation. He hurried down the terminal corridor toward the security checkpoint, where he knew he'd find Jimmy waiting on the other side. Sure enough, as Corey stepped out of the terminal, there Jimmy was, beaming broadly. Corey rushed into his outstretched arms. "Oh my God, I missed you so much!"

Jimmy squeezed Corey tightly, pulling him firmly against his hard chest. "Mmm, I missed you too.... Oh, gosh, how I missed ya." Corey wanted to do so much more than hug him, but restrained himself, and when he finally pulled back from the embrace, Jimmy spun him around to face the boy who was standing beside him.

"Corey, I'd like you to meet my kid brother. This here's Charlie. Charlie, this is Corey."

"Pleasure to meet ya, Mr. Corey," he said, nodding.

Corey grinned and stepped up to him. "I've heard a million things about you, Charlie. All wonderful." He extended his arms and hugged the boy affectionately.

Charlie was smiling as he looked into Corey's eyes. "I've heard a lot about you too, Mr. Corey," he said. "You're all Jimmy can talk about."

Corey turned to Jimmy and saw his face was becoming scarlet. "Oh, I bet. He's probably telling you what a pain in the butt I was in New York."

"Yeah, more or less," Charlie said, laughing.

"And you really do look a lot like our friend Tristan, the kid who was in New York with us."

"That's funny," Charlie said. "Jimmy told me about that. Guess it means I have a twin."

Although Charlie did bear a striking resemblance to Tristan, he was a couple inches shorter, and his face was a little bit thinner. It was their hair and eyes that made them look so similar. Corey wondered how Tristan was doing after his experience in New York. It was kind of sad that he'd probably never see him again.

The threesome made their way to baggage claim to retrieve Corey's luggage, and Charlie pretty much chattered the entire way. They lived in a small town about an hour north of Lexington. The town, Owenton, was about twenty minutes closer to Lexington than it was to Louisville, which was why Jimmy had suggested Corey try flying into that airport. The Lexington airport was also much smaller.

Charlie was excited about being able to make the hour-long trip with his big brother. He went on about it as if it were a great adventure. Knowing a bit of their family's history, Corey understood why Charlie appreciated little things like that. He'd spent many weeks—months on end, actually—imprisoned in hospital rooms and his own bedroom, even.

"Congratulations on winning," Charlie said to Corey. "I knew Jimmy would. I just knew it all along."

"Come on, motormouth," Jimmy said as he hoisted Corey's suitcase off the conveyor. He placed it beside him and then picked up a smaller bag, also Corey's, and handed it to his little brother. "You carry that one."

"I can handle the bigger one," Charlie protested.

"Didn't say you couldn't, but I already got the big one, so just take that one and shut your trap." He winked at Corey as he lightly slugged his little brother's arm.

When they got to the parking lot, Jimmy pointed out his car. "Sorry, it's not a real classy ride." It was an older model Dodge Charger.

"What are you talking about, Jimmy? This baby is sweet. It looks like the General Lee. Remember? From *Dukes of Hazzard*."

"You've seen *Dukes of Hazzard*?" Charlie asked, astonished. "I didn't think Yankees got that on their TVs."

Corey burst out laughing. "Well, do the doors open, or do we have to jump through the windows?"

Jimmy opened the passenger door for him. "Just 'cause we live in the South don't mean we're all rednecks."

Corey climbed inside as Jimmy threw the luggage in the trunk. He and Charlie entered the car from the driver's side, and Charlie slid into the backseat. "I don't care if y'all wanna kiss," Charlie said. "It don't bother me."

Corey expected to see Jimmy's face redden again, but when he looked over at him, he was smiling sweetly. "Okay," Corey said, then he leaned across the seat and kissed Jimmy squarely on the lips.

"Just please don't be making out in public," Charlie said. "It's annoying. I hate that, even when straight people do it."

"Point taken," Corey replied. "I agree. So how'd you get to be so cool, Charlie?"

"You mean 'cause it don't bother me to see two guys kiss?"

"Yeah, among other things."

"Jimmy says he loves you. He's my brother, and I want him to be happy, so why would it bother me to see him kiss the person he loves?"

"Can you please come home with me and talk to my mother?" Corey asked.

During the weeks following the elimination round, Corey and Jimmy had communicated every single day. They used text messaging, phone calls, and the Internet; but in spite of this steady flow of conversation, they still had a lot to say to each other. Corey told Jimmy about his morning, how he'd gotten Megan to drive him to Traverse City to catch his flight before the break of dawn. He told him how excited he'd been, and that he couldn't believe he was actually here in Kentucky. All he'd thought about since the day they left New York was being with Jimmy again.

Both Corey and Jimmy had received a lot of local attention in their hometowns when they returned in September. Everyone had wanted to know how they did in the competition. Although they were not allowed to give specific results, they could say it had gone well and that they'd be going to Hollywood in January.

People who were fans of the show knew what this meant—that they had made it into the Top Twenty-four. But neither of them were allowed to give interviews to the media, and for the most part they had to return to their normal lives, at least for the three-month period that led up to their trip to Hollywood.

"You guys do realize you're gonna be competing against each other," Charlie pointed out.

"So?" Jimmy said. "What's your point?"

"Well, I dunno. Don't you think that might be a bit... awkward?"

"We're both going to do our best," Corey said.

"And we both would be happy to see the other win," Jimmy said.

"Speak for yourself!" Corey joked. "No just kidding. Jimmy's right. I'd be just as happy to see him win as I would be to win myself."

"What would really suck is if one of us gets voted off early and the other doesn't," Jimmy said.

"What if you make it all the way to the end and you're the last two contestants?"

"That'd be cool," Corey said.

"Would it? Think about it," Charlie said. "It's something you've both dreamed about your whole lives. Then you are almost there... you've almost reached that goal. That prize that had always seemed unattainable. It's right there before your eyes, but the person who snatches it from you is the guy you love the most. I think that'd be really hard." He was leaning forward, his chin resting on the seat between them.

"Charlie, you think too much," Jimmy said. "Of course we'd both like to win, but if you love someone, you're happy to see them achieve their dreams."

"Even if it means you don't achieve yours?"

"No matter what happens, I'll always have my music, and I think just being in this competition is gonna help me. I'm already getting offers to perform all over the place."

"Well, I think you got to have the right attitude," Charlie said. "If you don't want to win more than anything, you probably won't. And I think if both of you feel this way, it could be hard...."

Corey thought about Charlie's words. In a way, the kid made sense. He did love Jimmy and would be very happy for him if he won the contest, but on the other hand, this had been his dream his whole life. He'd fantasized about being on *Superstar* long before he'd ever met Jimmy. It would be excruciating if he had to choose between his dream and Jimmy. He was just glad he didn't. They'd both made it into the Top Twenty-four, and now all they had to do was give their best performances. They both already were winners.

"Charlie, we're both winners already. We both want to win the contest, but all we can really do is give it our all. It's gonna be up to the voters to choose the singer they like best."

"So you're saying that if it did get down to just the two of you, and you were competing only against each other, you wouldn't be glad if the other made a mistake or screwed up somehow?"

"No, Charlie," Jimmy said. He was starting to sound irritated. "Both of us are going to make mistakes. We're human, and no one is perfect. If Corey happened to mess up his song while competing against me, I'd feel terrible for him. I'd never be happy about something like that."

"Well, even when I was in school sports, playing against my best friends, I wanted to win at all costs," Charlie said. "Maybe it's just my competitive nature."

"I don't think this is exactly the same thing," Corey said. "Like I said, we're both already winners. Regardless of who comes out on top, we're both likely to benefit from the competition. Sometimes the runners-up have far more successful careers than the person who technically won."

"Say what you want," Charlie replied, "but I just know that even though there is no one on earth that I love more than my big brother, if

I were competing against him in a contest, I'd want to win. When it comes to competition, it's not a matter of love… it's war."

"Well, that's how you've got to think of it," Jimmy said. "We have competed against each other a lot in our lives. We've played games, sports, even made bets with each other. We do both want to win, but in the end, what is more important? Winning or being brothers?"

Charlie smiled and placed his hand on his brother's shoulder. "That's a dumb question," he said.

"Exactly. And your question to us is the same way. Corey and I love each other, and that's much more important than winning."

"Oh," Charlie said jokingly, "I was gonna say kicking your ass was way more important than being your brother."

"I'll pull this car over," Jimmy threatened, "and we'll see who kicks whose butt."

"WELCOME to Owenton, population thirteen hundred," Jimmy said as they passed through the city limits. There wasn't much to the town itself, but Corey didn't mind. It made him feel right at home. His northern Michigan town was about the same size, though with a slightly larger population. "Mama's making lunch for us, but if y'all want to get some snacks for later, we can. I gotta stop here at this gas station."

"Doritos!" Charlie declared.

"Boy, you're gonna turn into a Dorito," Jimmy scolded. He winked at Corey. Corey loved the dynamic that existed with Jimmy and his little brother. He wished that he and his sister shared a rapport like that. Lanie and he had been close when they were younger, but not so much anymore.

As they stepped into the service station, Corey felt like he'd gone back in time. It was not laid out at all like a modern convenience store. Instead it looked like an old mercantile or something. "This is more like a little general store," Corey observed. "They have everything in here.

Sugar and flour. Breakfast cereal. Fresh-made deli subs. Even fishing equipment."

"And live bait," Jimmy added. "This here's where we buy our worms 'fore we go out fishin'."

"Seriously?" Corey said, laughing.

"Y'all want some soda?" Jimmy asked.

"Sure," Corey said. "But when you come to Michigan, we don't call it soda."

"What do y'all call it up there?" Charlie asked, intrigued.

"Pop," Corey said.

The brothers laughed. "That there is what y'all call your daddy in these parts."

The boys loaded up their arms with a few types of chips and sodas and made their way up to the counter.

"Afternoon, Mr. Jimmy," the middle-aged woman behind the counter greeted him. "Charlie." She nodded toward the younger boy.

"Afternoon, Miss Evelyn. I'd like you to meet my friend Corey. He's from Michigan, and he was in that singing competition with me. Remember when I went to New York a few weeks back?"

"Ah, I sure do. Well, it's a pleasure to meet ya. You gonna be on TV too like Jimmy here?"

"Yes, ma'am," Corey said. "We both have to go to California in January for the rest of the competition."

"We are so proud of our Jimmy," Evelyn said. "To think a local boy from our own hometown has made it so far. You know, Jimmy, this whole town is pullin' for ya. When I see you step foot in my very own store, my heart just a races. I feel like I'm in the presence of greatness."

Jimmy was blushing, but he nodded politely at the matronly lady. "Why, thank you, Miss Evelyn. That there means a lot to me, and I feel a bit like I'm in the presence of greatness myself. You run a fine establishment here."

"Oh, *pfft*," she said, waving her hand dismissively. "But thank you, Jimmy. And good luck to both of ya. No offense, Mr. Corey, but I'll be pulling for Mr. Jimmy."

"None taken, ma'am," Corey said. "I'm pulling for him myself... I mean I'm pulling for both of us."

"There ya go," she said.

It wasn't until they'd chatted at least a good ten minutes that Miss Evelyn finally began ringing up their purchases. "Oh, I almost forgot," Jimmy said. "I need to get some gas. Forty dollars, please."

"I just can't believe how friendly people are here," Corey said as they got back to the car.

"It's called southern hospitality," Charlie said.

"It's a far cry from New York City," Jimmy added.

"Well, I like it," Corey said.

"If you liked Miss Evelyn, wait'l ya meet Mama. She'll be kissin' all over your face," Charlie warned.

"Mama gets a little emotional sometimes," Jimmy said.

"I think I'm gonna like your mama."

"See that building there with the 'Quick Lube' sign? That there's where I work."

"Wow, at least your town has one," Corey quipped. "The town I'm from has one quick lube and one McDonald's, and about forty churches."

"We have a lot of churches too, but we also got a Burger King."

Jimmy pumped the gas, and the boys got back in the car. "There's a grocery store here, down on the next street, and we have a hardware, couple diners, and a bar. Frankfort's a little over a half-hour's drive from here if we need anything else."

"Daddy works in Cranetown," Charlie said. "An hour's drive from here."

"Really? He drives that far every day?"

"He works in the Toyota factory there," Jimmy explained. He's a foreman. It's a good job, but when he got the job, he didn't want to move the whole family. Daddy grew up here. Says it's worth the drive to live in his hometown and raise his family here."

"What about you?" Corey asked. "How do you like it here?"

Jimmy glanced over to him, then looked back to the road. His expression pensive, he lowered his voice. "I really do love it here. I love my family, my hometown...."

"But...?"

"But sometimes I want more. Ya know what I mean? I want to see more of the world, go places, do things that I can't do in this little town."

"Like being on *America's Next Superstar*?"

"Yeah, like that." He winked at Corey, then slid his hand across the seat and rested it on Corey's leg. "Know what I really want?"

"What?"

"I'd love to do some traveling. Make a living with my music, but have a home of my own to always come back to. If by the grace of God I'm successful, I'd like to make things right with my folks. Pay them back for all they done for me over the years, and then get myself my own place."

"You have a big heart, Jimmy," Corey said, placing his hand atop Jimmy's and squeezing it.

Jimmy responded by massaging Corey's thigh with his thumb and fingers. "This right here's our humble home," he said, pulling into a long, gravel driveway. Jimmy started laughing. "And that there's Mama, waitin' for us on the front porch."

Corey peered out the window at the modest, ranch-style home. It was nice—very homey—but far from palatial. It was just an average home, typical for the all-American family, and Corey could easily visualize Jimmy growing up here.

Jimmy laid on the horn as they approached the house, and his mother stepped off the porch and approached the car. The three boys piled out, and Mrs. Sawyer stepped over to Corey. "You must be Corey," she said. "I'm so excited to finally meet you." She wrapped him in a warm embrace, kissing the side of his face.

"I told ya Mama would kiss all over yer face," Charlie said.

"You hush," she said. "I can kiss who I wanna kiss. My oh my, you're the skinniest little thing. Worse than Jimmy!"

"I'm sure you'll fatten him up while he's here," Jimmy joked. "You got a whole seven days to make sure he gets his fill."

"Well, I got dinner waitin'," she said.

Corey couldn't believe how warmly he'd been accepted into Jimmy's family. He'd feared it would be awkward, that he and Jimmy might have to hide their relationship, but so far it had been exactly the opposite. If only his own family was as accepting of him as was Jimmy's. Corey was beginning to worry how Jimmy would feel when he came to Michigan. He knew his mother and sister would not give Jimmy anywhere near the warm welcome that Corey had received in Kentucky.

"*This* is lunch?" Corey exclaimed when he looked at the table. It seemed more like Thanksgiving dinner. There was a huge platter of fried chicken, a heaping plate of cornbread, homemade stuffing, creamed green beans, corn on the cob, and an enormous strawberry-rhubarb pie.

"Mama cooks enough to feed an army," Jimmy explained.

"Now, I don't usually make such a big meal for lunch, but this here was a special occasion."

Mrs. Sawyer grilled Corey with questions throughout the meal, asking him how he'd liked his experience in New York. She asked him about his family and his hometown, what he wanted to do with his life besides singing. She was about the sweetest and most genuine person Corey had ever met other than Jimmy. He could see where Jimmy got his manners.

"Mrs. Sawyer, I think this was the best meal I've ever had," Corey said truthfully.

"Now you stop," she said. "That there is such a sweet thing to say."

"We're lucky," Jimmy interjected. "Mama's a great cook."

"I'll help clean up," Corey volunteered, pushing his chair back.

"No, no, you boys head on downstairs. I'll take care of this mess."

"Are you sure?"

"I'm absolutely positive," she said. "You're our guest."

"I think I'm gonna go lie down," Charlie said. "I'm a little tired."

"Are you okay?" Jimmy said, suddenly looking worried.

"I'm fine," he assured everyone. "It was an early morning... lot of excitement. I'm just gonna take a little nap."

Corey looked into Jimmy's face, which registered his genuine concern. Mrs. Sawyer got up from the table and retrieved something from the kitchen. "You didn't take your noon meds," she said, handing some pills to Charlie. "Do you need a pain pill?"

"No!" Charlie responded, shaking his head. "I'll be too drowsy. I'm just gonna lie down a few minutes."

She stood there as Charlie swallowed his medication, and then she led him down the hallway to his room.

"Will he be okay?" Corey asked Jimmy.

"He gets tired easy, after the surgery. Going with me to Lexington was quite an adventure for him."

"Wow," Corey said. "It makes me feel bad. I should have just rented a car...."

"Nah," Jimmy said. "It ain't your fault Charlie wanted to come with me. It's probably good for him, actually. The more he gets out and does things, the stronger he'll get. Come on, I'll show you my room downstairs."

Corey followed Jimmy down the hall and then into a stairwell that led to the lower level. At the base of the stairs, they stepped into a large open room which appeared to be like a family or entertainment room. Corey's eyes immediately went to the piano.

"Wow, you have a piano," Corey said.

"Do you play?"

Corey nodded. "I've been playing since I was in the first grade, but I always had to practice at school. We don't have our own piano at home."

Beside the piano was an array of other musical instruments, including Jimmy's guitar. "This here is where I write most of my songs."

"Really? You write your own music?"

"I wrote you a song too," Jimmy said, stepping closer to Corey.

"I love you so much," Corey whispered, only a split second before he felt the heat of Jimmy's lips crushing his own. Corey closed his eyes and wrapped his arms around Jimmy's broad shoulders, savoring the taste and smell of the man who was now the center of his universe.

"Come on," Jimmy said, "I'll show you my room." He took Corey by the hand and led him to his bedroom. And that's when they really got serious about kissing.

LATER that evening, after Jimmy's father got home from work, the family had a big supper. Corey was anything but hungry, after having indulged at lunch. Jimmy explained to him that lunches were typically not so bountiful, but it was his mom's way of welcoming Corey to their home.

Jimmy's dad had a far more reserved personality than the rest of the family. He was not unfriendly, but he wasn't talkative the way Charlie and Mrs. Sawyer were. Some extended family—cousins, aunts, and uncles—and a few neighbors came over later in the evening, and they all gathered downstairs.

The lower level had a sliding glass door that led out to a large patio, just off the family room. This allowed guests to mingle indoors and out. Corey was pleased to discover that Mr. Sawyer also had some musical talent. He played guitar, and soon the three of them were entertaining the crowd. Corey played piano while Jimmy and his dad were on guitars. Jimmy and Corey took turns singing, and sometimes sang together. With some songs, everyone joined in. Mr. Sawyer claimed he didn't have a singing voice, but from what Corey could hear, he did all right.

The celebration continued well into the late hours of the evening, in spite of the fact that it was a weeknight. Charlie appeared to be feeling much better, and after his nap and a hearty supper, he seemed to have regained energy.

Finally, when everyone had cleared out for the evening, Jimmy's parents informed the boys they were going to call it a night. Charlie insisted he wasn't tired yet and turned on the big-screen TV in the family room. Corey and Jimmy sat down with him as he surfed the channels. Once he settled on a movie, he quickly dozed off, slumping onto the leather cushion. Jimmy waited about ten minutes, and then very quietly walked over and scooped the boy up into his arms and carried him upstairs to his bedroom.

When Jimmy returned, Corey was still sitting on the sofa, waiting for him. "Where am I sleeping?" Corey asked.

"Officially or actually?" Jimmy asked.

"Actually…."

"With me, of course. Officially you're in the guest bedroom across the hall."

"Ah, and we're not gonna get caught?"

"You've met my folks," Jimmy said. "Do you really think they'd care? I'm sure they know we're sleeping together."

"If you want, I could go to bed in my own room and wait for you to sneak over in the middle of the night to take advantage of me."

Jimmy sat down on the couch beside him. "I can't wait that long," he said. "I wanna take advantage of you now, not in the middle of the night." He leaned in and planted a kiss on Corey's expectant lips. "And in the middle of the night too."

"Mmm," Corey moaned. "That was sweet, the way you carried your brother to his room."

"Like this?" Jimmy slid an arm around Corey's shoulder while scooping his other arm beneath his knees and then quickly hoisted him from the sofa.

"I feel like a bride."

"And you're about to be deflowered."

"Deflower me… please," Corey whispered.

THURSDAY of that week was Thanksgiving, and it came as no surprise to Corey that it was another enormous meal. This time, instead of it being the solitary effort of Jimmy's mom, the dinner included dishes from numerous family members. The entire extended family was there—aunts, uncles, cousins, grandparents, spouses, kids—a total of thirty-four guests. Not one of them said a negative word to Corey. They all accepted him as Jimmy's friend, though he did get a little bit of ribbing for being Jimmy's competitor on *Superstar*.

As hectic as it was Thanksgiving morning, by late afternoon everyone was lethargic. Overstuffed and drowsy, several guests gathered around the big screen downstairs to watch the football games. About half the extended family said their goodbyes and took off for the day.

"Come on," Jimmy said, "let's go for a walk."

"Good idea," Corey agreed. "If I sit here much longer, I'm gonna be asleep."

They walked for a couple hundred feet, and when finally the house behind them was out of sight, Jimmy took Corey's hand. "Three more days," he said. "That's all I have left with you."

"And then it'll just be a month… and you'll come see me."

"I can't wait." He squeezed Corey's hand. "I wanna show you something. See that house up ahead?"

"Yeah."

"That's my granddaddy's."

"The one I met today?"

"Yeah. He's ninety-four. He's leaving me that house when he dies."

"Wow. That's nice, but why you?"

"We've always been close, and I'm the first grandson. Granddad could live to be a hundred twenty, though. He's been healthy as a horse his whole life."

"Maybe you'll be rich and famous and won't even need the house by that time."

"I'll never be too rich or too famous to live in Granddad's house. That there is where I wanna raise my family."

"Your family?" Corey asked. "You want kids?"

"Don't you?"

"Uh… I never really thought about it. I guess I just don't picture myself as ever being able to get married."

"We could go back to New York to get married," Jimmy said.

Corey stopped in his tracks. "We?"

"I'm sorry." Jimmy suddenly appeared regretful, as if he feared he'd said the wrong thing.

"Jimmy, don't be sorry." Corey's voice was barely audible. He was choking up. "Yes, we could go to New York to get married… or Vermont or Connecticut. There are a bunch of states now. But Jimmy, does this mean you're proposing?"

Jimmy pulled Corey into him, kissing him tenderly on the lips. "Consider it a preproposal, I guess. No, this is not the way I wanna propose. I ain't even met your mama or your family yet."

Corey felt the sting of the hot tears streaming down his cheeks. "So if this is a preproposal, do you need a preanswer?"

"Not if you're not ready…."

"I'm not ready to go home. I'm not ready to leave you again. I love it here, and I love your family…."

"But this isn't exactly real life," Jimmy said. "It's usually a lot more boring. I'm usually working nine or ten hours a day. We usually don't have all this company and all these huge dinners."

"I don't think life with you would ever be boring to me."

"I'll take you horseback riding tomorrow," Jimmy promised. "And we're doin' a show tomorrow night at the civic center. It's to raise money for Julia Brentworth. She's only sixteen and has cancer."

"Oh, wow."

"You can sing with me."

"I'd like that. I'd like that a lot, and I think I'd be fine with your real life."

"Corey, even if I succeed, I'm always gonna just be a country boy. You're probably going places I never even dreamed of. You're gonna be a superstar for real. I'm so afraid that my boring, country lifestyle is not gonna fit...."

"Jimmy, I should be the one who's worried. What you have here is heaven. When you see my hometown and meet my family, you'll understand. I came out to my mom a long time ago. I always thought she was fine, that she had no problem with it, but she does. All this time she was just pretending to support me, but she really thought I'd outgrow being gay."

"Lots of folks are like that. Especially round here," Jimmy said. "I'm just lucky. Mama and Daddy almost lost one son. They aren't about to lose the other to prejudice. I think there are people everywhere who are like that. We hear it a lot, people sayin' it's a sin. Some say it's just a choice. Give your mama time. She'll come around; I know she will."

"I guess we should focus on getting through the competition before we make any plans," Corey said, "but I know I don't wanna live my life without you. Somehow, some way, we've got to be together. And no matter who wins or loses, you'll always be my Superstar."

TWELVE

"WHAT do you mean, he can't stay here? Mom, he's already got his plane ticket. He'll be here in four days!"

"Corey, you're asking me to do something I just can't do. I'm not comfortable having him in my house. You're old enough to do what you want, and I'll always love you. But that doesn't mean I have to condone your lifestyle."

Corey's jaw came unhinged as he listened to the unbelievable statements his own mother was making. "Mom, you already know the lifestyle that I live. It's the same lifestyle that you and Lanie have. I'm not some sort of circus freak just because I'm gay."

"I wish you'd never gotten involved in this contest... this *Superstar* thing. It's changed you, Corey. You came back from New York, and now all of a sudden you want to shove this homosexuality down everyone's throat. This is northern Michigan—*not* New York City."

It seemed every time he and his mother were in the kitchen together there was an argument. He looked up at the wall clock, noticing that it was past midnight, and wondered if it'd be too late to call Jimmy. What was he going to tell him? Jimmy couldn't cancel his trip, not this late.

"Mom, when I went down there for Thanksgiving, Jimmy's whole family welcomed me. They accepted me just like I was one of their own, but you won't even let Jimmy sleep in your house."

"You have no idea what it's like. I go to work every day. To the supermarket. The bank. People stop me and ask me about my son, the one on *America's Next Superstar*. They say, 'You must be so proud,' and I don't know how to answer them."

"Maybe you could say, 'Thank you', or even, 'Yes, I'm very proud.' The problem is, you're not. You're not proud of me at all. You're ashamed. You're embarrassed that your son is a *fag*, and now the whole world is gonna see."

"I love you, Corey," she said, choking back tears. "I will always love you, no matter what. But you've chosen a life I cannot condone."

"Look, Jimmy's coming here, and I'm spending New Year's with him. If you want me to be a part of this family, you've got to accept me for who I am and respect the person that I love. If not, I'll stay with Jimmy in his hotel room, and I'll move out of your house when he goes back home."

"Corey, don't be ridiculous. You know you can't afford to live on your own...."

"The college has a dormitory. I can get in there during semester break and stay till I save up enough for an apartment. Or maybe I'll just move to Kentucky!" Tears were now streaming down his mother's cheeks. Corey was on the verge of tears himself, because he was so angry. "You say you love me, Mom, but you have a piss-poor way of showing it."

He stormed off to his bedroom, slamming the door behind him. He did call Jimmy, in spite of the fact it was so late, and Jimmy's calm, soothing voice made him feel better. He assured Corey it was going to be all right. He'd be glad to pay for a hotel room, and that might be better anyway.

Four days later, Megan drove Corey to the Traverse City airport, where they picked up Jimmy. She dropped them off at the Best Western motel, where they stayed the next three days. They spent most of their time by the indoor pool and walked downtown to look at all the stores which still had up their Christmas decorations. Jimmy had never seen that much snow, so Corey had to initiate him by starting a snowball fight. They went to the gay bar on New Year's Eve. They weren't old enough to drink but were allowed entry with a hand stamp.

Jimmy's visit was way too short, but when he left they knew it'd only be three more weeks until they were together in California. During that interim period, Corey moved his belongings to a dorm room. He wasn't even sure if he'd be back by the end of the semester. If he succeeded in the contest, he could be in Hollywood until as late as June. All of the new classes he'd enrolled in were online courses, and he was using his financial aid to pay for his housing.

There was no big send-off on the day of his departure. Although he was nervous, the whole thing seemed anticlimactic. Megan dropped him off at the airport and gave him a hug and kiss goodbye. His arrival in Hollywood was starkly different than the trip to New York. This time he was treated like a celebrity. A limousine transferred him to his hotel, and he was given a private room. The room was much nicer than what he and Jimmy had shared in New York. This room was a suite and had its own kitchen and living room, and there was even a Jacuzzi in the bathroom.

Corey flopped down on the sofa, sprawling out. It would be another eight hours until Jimmy arrived, so he decided to sleep off some of his jet lag.

Just as he dozed off, he was startled awake by a knock at the door. He got up and stumbled over to open the door. His jaw nearly hit the floor when he saw who was standing before him.

"Hello, Corey," Reuben said, "welcome to Hollywood."

JIMMY'S adrenaline was surging, not only because he'd just gotten off the plane and was on his way to the hotel where he'd begin preparing for the *America's Next Superstar* show, but also because he was only minutes away from being with the one person he loved more than life itself. Back in Kentucky, on Thanksgiving Day, he'd promised Corey that when the time was right, he would propose to him the proper way.

In his pocket, he was concealing a very special package. He didn't know for sure exactly when he would pull it out, but sometime before he left Hollywood, he would drop to bended knee, pull the tiny box from his pocket, and slip the ring on Corey's finger. The contest was exciting, and he'd love to win. He'd love it if Corey won too. But the bottom line was that winning was secondary. He'd already won the biggest prize, and no contest was ever going to change that.

He looked at his watch and wondered if he should try calling Corey's cell phone. It was after midnight, but Corey had arrived eight hours prior. He'd have had time to nap. Jimmy decided to text him. Hopefully he'd respond, but if not, he'd just wait till morning to see him.

Wait till morning to see him? Jimmy laughed at the ridiculous thought. Of course he wouldn't wait until morning. If Corey was tired and needed to sleep, that was fine, but he'd be there beside him, holding him against his warm body.

He picked up his phone and dialed Corey's number. After three rings, Corey answered.

"Hey, did you make it?" Corey said. Jimmy knew immediately that something was wrong. He could tell by the tone of Corey's voice, and he sounded like he might have been crying.

"What's wrong?" Jimmy asked, concerned.

"Oh, nothing. I'm just tired."

"I figured ya might be. Jet lag and all."

"I think I'm gonna go to bed," Corey said. "Call it an early night."

"I should be there in a few minutes. I'm at the airport waiting for my ride."

"Oh, that might be awhile. Listen, just get checked in, and I'll see you in the morning."

"What's your room number?"

"I'll talk to you tomorrow sometime." The call ended.

"Hello?" Jimmy stared at his phone, puzzled. That was crazy. He'd spoken to Corey on the phone every single day since September, and not once had their conversation ended without them telling each other, "I love you."

Something was definitely wrong. Jimmy wondered if maybe Corey'd had another fight with his mother. He had to find out. He couldn't stand having Corey upset like that. He'd go to the hotel and get checked in and then find Corey. He wasn't about to let his Corey spend his first night in Hollywood alone.

COREY really didn't care one way or the other if he won the contest. He'd decided a long time ago that the fame and money were not his true ambitions. Sure, the national media attention would help. It could catapult him to stardom. If he were lucky, he'd be able to make a career of his music alone.

But what Corey really wanted was that farmhouse in Kentucky. He wanted a life with Jimmy, maybe even a family someday. He wanted a family like Jimmy's that loved and accepted him for who he was. He could picture it, living in a small town like that with the man of his dreams. Jimmy, with his deep baritone voice and broad shoulders, was Corey's living, breathing dream come true.

He sat on the couch and stared at the package in his hands. It was an eight-by-ten manila envelope, and it contained photos. Lots of photos. And they were all of Jimmy.

Corey wasn't a prude. He'd never expected that Jimmy was perfect. Didn't everyone have secrets? Didn't everyone have at least some skeleton in their closet? The hard thing for Corey to swallow was the fact that Jimmy obviously had lied to him. He'd told Corey that night they made love for the first time, that Corey was his first.

Well, no, Corey obviously was not Jimmy's first. Could it be that the photos were photoshopped? Maybe, but how would they know that Jimmy had the heart tattoo on his upper bicep with his mama's initials? How would they know the exact size and shape of Jimmy's, um... privates? That expression on his face when he reached orgasm—Corey had seen it dozens of times—and it was also there in the photos.

So Jimmy had been a porn star. Was it really that big a deal?

That fact alone would probably not have been enough to devastate Corey. They could have worked it out. Corey was pretty sure that the reason Jimmy had never told him this detail of his past was because he wasn't proud of it. He was probably embarrassed. And when he told Corey that he was his first, maybe he meant that he was the first person he'd really and truly "made love to." Wasn't that more than just fucking?

But what was most troubling to Corey was the fact that Reuben had made it very clear that the photos would be released to the media. The results would be catastrophic if this happened. All of Jimmy's dreams would be shattered. His family would be mortified. His brother would be utterly devastated, and Jimmy would be immediately kicked off *America's Next Superstar*.

The only option that Corey had was to comply with Reuben's wishes. He had to report to Reuben's room at midnight, and any other time that Reuben beckoned him, from now until the contest was over. If he failed to do as ordered, Reuben would ruin Jimmy.

Tears streamed down Corey's face as he stared at the images. It was so ironic, because if Corey had seen these photos before meeting Jimmy, he'd have found them extremely hot. They *were* hot, because Jimmy was hot. But at this stage, they felt like a betrayal. It felt to Corey as if Jimmy had lied and had cheated on him. He couldn't get it out of his mind, seeing Jimmy with these other guys—several other guys, and in several positions, doing several different things.

After Jimmy called and said he'd made it to the airport, Corey hung up the phone. Slowly he pushed himself up off the sofa and padded his way down the corridor into the bathroom, where he then showered and got dressed. He turned off the lights and closed the door behind him, then headed down the hall to the elevator.

JIMMY got checked into the hotel and dropped off his suitcases in his room. He checked his appearance in the mirror and splashed on some cologne. He then took the elevator back downstairs to the lobby. He waited patiently until the desk clerk who'd checked him in moments before left the front desk area. Jimmy stepped up to the counter, and another clerk acknowledged him. "May I help you, sir?"

"Uh, yeah. I feel like an idiot. I locked my room key in my room...."

"Not a problem. sir. Happens all the time. What's your name and room number?"

"Corey Dunham... and well, I can't remember the exact number. I'm sorry... uh... it was a long flight."

"Four thirty-seven," the clerk said with a smile. He handed Jimmy another key.

"Oh, thank you so much. You're a lifesaver."

Corey was probably sleeping, but Jimmy would just slip in and surprise him. He'd curl up next to him in bed and hold Corey tight. He could picture it now: Corey would feel his warm body beside him and would curl up in his arms and they'd snuggle.

When Jimmy pushed the door open and stepped into Corey's room, it was dark. Yeah, he must be in bed already. He felt against the wall for a light switch and turned it on. A lamp on the opposite side of the room came on. Jimmy closed the door behind him and stepped inside. Quietly he made his way down the hall toward the bedroom.

Once inside he saw the room was empty, and the bed hadn't been slept in. He flipped on the overhead light and saw Corey's suitcases in the corner. Well, he definitely had the right room, but where was Corey? Maybe he'd gone down to get a bite to eat.

Jimmy pulled out his phone and called Corey's number. As it rang, Jimmy heard Corey's ringtone in the living room of the suite. Corey must not have taken his phone with him, wherever he'd gone. Yeah, he must not have gone far. Probably to get a soda or something. Silly guy, he should have just ordered room service. It was included.

He headed back out to the living room and took a seat on the sofa. There it was—Corey's phone. It was sitting there atop a manila envelope. Jimmy picked up the phone and looked at the missed call from himself. He smiled. He then grabbed the envelope. He probably shouldn't look. Really, it was none of his business, but he doubted that Corey would mind. They really didn't keep any secrets from each other, and besides, it felt like pictures. Corey was probably planning to show them to him anyway.

As Jimmy pulled out the large glossy photos, his felt the blood drain from his face as his jaw fell open. This explained the why Corey had been crying, why he'd hung up on him. But how? Where had Corey found the photos?

COREY felt too defeated even to cry. The mixture of disgust, humiliation, shame, and self-hatred was crippling. It was quite literally a matter of sensory and emotional overload. What he wanted to do was simply find a place to hide—a hole to crawl in and never come out. Unfortunately, he didn't have that option. Tomorrow would be a very busy day.

Superstar was already broadcasting the second week of their preseason episodes. Last week they'd featured the auditions in Louisville. This week it would be Detroit, and Corey's audition might, in fact, be one of the segments they elected to air. The contestants would have only two weeks to prepare for the live shows. This would include a very tight schedule that included rehearsals, meetings with voice coaches, media consultants, wardrobe and hair specialists, and a multitude of public appearances. All of the Top Twenty-four contestants would be attending press conferences and giving television interviews. Some would be selected to star in commercials for sponsoring companies. Some would be making public service announcements. They all would participate in the filming of music videos.

Regardless of the vote tallies and who won the competition, they all would be terribly busy. It was now after three in the morning, which gave Corey a mere four hours to get some sleep. He was thankful he'd had the short nap yesterday evening.

Worst of all, he'd likely have to face Jimmy. It was going to be difficult. As hard as it was to get the images of those photos out of his head, it was even harder to forget what he'd experienced with Reuben. He felt so dirty, so defiled. What he needed was a shower—a long, hot shower to wash away Reuben's filth.

How could he ever be with Jimmy again? Maybe Corey would be able to forgive the indiscretions of Jimmy's past, but Corey could never expect Jimmy to forgive what he'd done tonight. What he'd allowed Reuben to do. What he'd willingly participated in.

Though he felt numb, the tears just seemed to flow on their own. It wasn't like an emotional breakdown. He wasn't sobbing. It was just a steady and heavy ache that he felt in the center of his chest, almost as if he were grieving. Maybe he was. Perhaps he was mourning the loss of his purity and innocence. What he'd shared with Jimmy had been beautiful, but his three hours with Reuben had been vile and disgusting.

It was dark in his room when he pushed the door open. He flipped on the light switch to turn on the lamp. As he did so, he noticed the body curled up on his sofa. Jimmy was lying there, holding the manila envelope against his chest.

As Jimmy sat up, Corey closed the door behind him. He stared at Jimmy, unable to speak.

"Where were you?" Jimmy whispered.

He shook his head and looked away. "It doesn't matter."

"Corey, we need to talk."

"You should go to your room. We have a long day tomorrow...."

"I'm sorry you found out this way," Jimmy said. "I wanted to tell you."

Corey looked down at the floor in front of his feet. He toed his shoes off and left them by the door. "Jimmy, in four hours we have to meet with all of the other contestants and the judges for a plenary session. I don't have the energy to discuss this now."

Jimmy stood up and stepped toward him. "Baby, you're crying...." He reached out to place his hand on Corey's shoulder, but Corey pulled away.

"I'm taking a shower and then going to bed for three hours. How'd you get in my room, by the way?"

"I lied to the desk clerk."

"That's not like you, Jimmy... to tell lies."

The hurt look on Jimmy's face made Corey regret his sarcasm.

"I know. It was wrong." Jimmy obviously wasn't referring to the lie he'd told the hotel staff. "It was when Charlie was so sick. I was giving my parents all of my paychecks, but it wasn't enough. They almost lost the house...."

"Jimmy, I wouldn't have cared what you did before you met me... if only you'd told me the truth."

"I'm so sorry," his voice cracked. "Corey, please forgive me." It broke Corey's heart, the way this man hung his head so shamefully, tears streaming down his cheeks.

"Are there any other secrets? Any other pictures you haven't told me about? Movies? Orgies? Drugs?"

He shook his head. "It was a movie. One movie, and they paid me a thousand dollars. They told me it would be distributed in Europe, that there was no chance my family or anyone I knew would ever see it."

Corey laughed, his tone laden with sarcasm. "Jimmy, haven't you ever heard of the Internet? How could you ever believe such bullshit?"

"I didn't care! Why would I? My brother was dying. My parents were penniless, three payments behind on their mortgage."

"But you said…." Corey was on the verge of losing it himself. He took a deep breath. "You said I was your first."

"You *were* my first, Corey. In that movie, I was acting. I was being paid money to be a fucking whore!" It was the first time Corey had ever heard him swear. "And you don't think that every day of my life I regret it? Sometimes you have to do things you're not proud of… to protect the people you love."

He wanted to embrace Jimmy, take him in his arms, and tell him he understood. He wanted to tell him everything was going to be all right, that there was nothing to forgive. He couldn't though. He couldn't return to Jimmy's arms when he knew he'd be returning over and over to Reuben's.

"Maybe I'm not man enough to understand that, Jimmy. I'm sorry."

"Please…," Jimmy pleaded. "Corey, please try to understand. I love you. I want to spend my life with you."

Corey walked into the kitchen area of his suite and opened the mini fridge. He took out a bottled water and unscrewed the cap. "Jimmy, I need some time."

"If anyone finds out about these pictures, I'll be out of the competition," Jimmy said. "I should probably just drop out, save myself the embarrassment. I'll do it and wait for you, Corey. I know you can win it."

"It would kill Charlie. It'd be devastating to your whole family."

"It'd be worse if they saw me disgraced… if they saw the photos."

"They won't see them. No one will ever see them…."

"You don't know that!"

"Jimmy, go back to your room and get some sleep. Get yourself ready for tomorrow, and then concentrate on the competition. That's what you're here for. Give me the time and space that I need, and we can sort this all out when it's over...."

"Thirteen weeks from now?"

"Thirteen weeks, thirteen days? What's it matter? We're both here until one of us gets voted off. All I know is I'm too tired to deal with this tonight, and so are you."

Jimmy walked out into the kitchen. "At least let me hold you...."

Corey placed the bottle on the countertop and slid into Jimmy's arms.

"I love you," Jimmy whispered, "and I'm so sorry."

"I love you too," Corey said with absolute sincerity. "But I have to go to bed."

Jimmy kissed him on the forehead. "Please... meet me for breakfast."

"Be here at seven."

"I'll be here at six forty-five."

THIRTEEN

COREY woke himself up screaming, or at first he thought he did. The alarm clock was also screaming. It was 6:30 a.m. His entire body was sore, and the lacerations on his back were raw. He felt like he needed another shower, at least to wake himself up, but it would be just too painful, so instead he splashed water on his face and brushed his teeth. Thankfully, Reuben would only be in Hollywood for one day. The judges flew in to attend the plenary session and a few opening-day events. They'd be back in two weeks when the live broadcasts began.

That would give Corey time to heal. Maybe it would give him time to think, as well. If there were some other way to protect Jimmy and his family—anything—he'd do it. He understood now why Tristan had been so demoralized. Of course the boy would be reluctant to ever testify against Reuben. His natural instinct would be to bury the memories, pretend the abuse had never happened. That is exactly how Corey now felt himself.

With the water running in the sink, Corey didn't hear the hotel room door open.

"Oh my God!" Jimmy gasped, standing in the bathroom doorway. "Corey, your back!"

Corey bit his lower lip and closed his eyes before turning to face him. "Have you ever heard of knocking?"

"Baby, what happened to you?" Jimmy asked, gasping. He stepped closer, reaching out with one hand.

Corey tried to back away, but he was standing against the sink. "You have your secrets. I have mine," he whispered. He snagged a towel from the rack on the opposite wall and patted it against his wet face.

"That man—the one who hurt Tristan—he did this to you." It was not a question.

"Jimmy, don't make this worse than it already is. Please."

He could see the rage rise in Jimmy's cheeks. His eyes were fire as he grabbed hold of Corey's shoulders. "How could you let him do this to you?" He sounded furious.

If Corey's emotions were not already so jumbled, he might have been frightened. Instead he was annoyed. "Me? How could *I* do this? Jimmy, how the fuck do you think I got the photos?"

Jimmy's grip on his shoulders tightened as he glared into Corey's face. "You had sex with him for the pictures?"

"Do you really think there'd be just one copy of those prints? No, I didn't have sex with Reuben for those disgusting pictures. I did what Reuben ordered me to do because I had no choice. Just like you sold your body for a thousand bucks because you had no choice."

"What are you talking about?" Jimmy screamed.

"Reuben brought me the fucking pictures! And if I don't give him what he wants whenever he fucking wants it, he's going to ruin you. He'll release the pictures to the media...."

The grip of Jimmy's fingers, which had been digging into Corey's shoulders, suddenly loosened. "He won't do that," Jimmy said. "It would be a bigger embarrassment to the show than to me...."

"In all honesty, I think you're right," Corey said, "or at least partially, but only if we make it through these first two weeks. Once they air your audition and reveal the Top Twenty-four to the nation, they won't want the scandal. Until then...."

"But, Corey, right now nobody even knows who I am. If he releases those pictures now, nobody will care."

"They'll have to kick you out, though. They'll send you packing, and your family will find out. And Charlie will be crushed...."

"No," Jimmy said, shaking his head, "you should have called his bluff. The worst he could have done was get me kicked off the show. If I go on to compete and get national media attention, he will always have this to hold over my head. He will be able to blackmail me, or you, to do whatever he wants."

"Jimmy, you don't get it." Frustrated, Corey released a sigh. "We made a deal. Reuben owns the video. He always has. It was his company you were working for. He is going to destroy the video and all the photos once the competition is over. The video was never released, and he owns the original tape."

"But if you don't do what he says...?"

"Then God knows what he'll do. He could wait till you're at the peak of your career and sell the video."

"Corey, let him do whatever he chooses to do. I'll call Daddy tonight and tell him everything. My family would never expect me to let him blackmail us."

"It's too late!" Corey exclaimed. "Why does it matter now? He's already had his fun with me."

"And I'll be next," Jimmy said. "This is a game he plays. It's about power. The only way to stop him is to call his bluff. Let him kick me off the show now, and this whole thing will go away."

"No! Jimmy, he's not even gonna be around after today. The judges are just here for the opening ceremony, then we won't see him for two weeks. Wait until the live shows begin to air and you're introduced to the nation as one of the Top Twenty-four. Then call his bluff."

"But then we'll never get the video from him."

"Unless...."

"What?"

"We've got to contact Tristan. We've got to get him to testify. Jimmy, I'm an adult, at least legally. Tristan is only seventeen, and if we can prove Reuben's been doing this all along...."

"Then what? We trade the evidence we have for the video? He'd be off scot-free, and next year he'd be doing the same thing all over again to another group of boys. We should have stopped him back in New York."

"Jimmy, call Tristan. Please. Maybe we can figure out a way to get the video and stop him from hurting anyone else."

THEY'D known their day would be busy, but Corey really hadn't anticipated how exhausting it would be. Throughout the day there were several events where he and Jimmy had to be separated, but Jimmy seemed obsessed with maintaining contact. Corey received multiple texts and phone calls during the times they had to head off in different directions. They did have lunch together, and they both had to attend the press conference and the photo ops that followed.

It was nine o'clock that night when they were finally done with all the scheduled activities. Jimmy followed Corey to his room. As soon as the door closed behind them, Corey felt Jimmy's arms around him.

"How's your back?" he asked. "Does it hurt?"

"Stings a little," Corey lied. The cuts and bruises he'd endured were excruciating, and his back had been on fire the whole day. "Maybe I'll take a cool shower."

"I'll put some cream on you," Jimmy offered.

Corey turned in Jimmy's arms so they were facing each other. Suddenly he was overwhelmed with emotion. "I thought when you found out what I'd done, you'd never be able to forgive me."

"How can you say that?" Jimmy choked, sounding equally emotional. "What did you do other than sacrifice yourself for me? Yeah, it makes me sick thinking about that evil man's hands on your body, thinking about the awful things he did to you, but you didn't do anything."

"You don't understand," Corey said. "Yes, it was awful. It was sick, but a lot of what he did was pleasurable, and then... then I felt guilty."

"You became aroused and hated yourself for it."

Corey nodded but didn't speak.

"You can't let yourself feel guilty, because none of this is your fault. Anyone can be aroused by stimulation, whether they want it or not. If you can forgive me for making that video, why wouldn't I be able to forgive—no, 'forgive' isn't even the right word. There is nothing to forgive. Why wouldn't I be able to accept that what you did was an act of love... for me?"

How was it that Corey had been so blessed, to have met a man like Jimmy? The floodgates opened, and he buried his face into Jimmy's hard chest, sobbing. Gently Jimmy's arms enfolded him, rocking him back and forth as he cried.

Sniffling, Corey pulled back to again look up into Jimmy's brown eyes. "I didn't even know you when you made that video. I don't have anything to forgive either. And to be honest, I've been thinking about those pictures. I'd like to try some of those positions."

Jimmy laughed.

"Haven't we already tried most of them?"

"It's so hot the way your rock-hard abs tighten when you're fucking. The expressions on your face. It's no wonder they chose you to be a porn star."

Jimmy cupped his hands around Corey's face, leaning in to kiss him. "You're so cute," he whispered. "I don't deserve you."

"Come on, let's go shower."

LATER, as Corey lay naked on the bed, on his stomach, Jimmy gently applied salve to his back. It felt good, and Jimmy's touch was tender and compassionate. Corey moaned and buried his head in the pillow.

"I've been thinkin' bout something," Jimmy said.

"Yeah?"

"Reuben's been doing this a long time. There's no question about that, and so there must be other victims. What if we look on the website for *America's Next Superstar* and see who some of the previous contestants were. Maybe we can find some who were also victimized."

"Yeah," Corey said, lifting his head slightly off the pillow. "Remember last year, there was that really young kid. Nate Carter. He was younger than Tristan—fifteen or sixteen."

"We should check him out. I bet we'll find contestants with that same look in every year."

"You think that's why he chose Tristan and me? Because of what we look like?"

"You're young-looking, like teen heartthrobs. I bet he likes your innocence."

"But I'm not as young-looking as Tristan."

"You're ten times better-looking than Tristan," Jimmy said as he continued to rub Corey's back.

"You're prejudiced," Corey complained. "It's not like you can give an unbiased opinion."

"I ain't prejudiced," Jimmy said. "I noticed how gorgeous you were the moment I laid eyes on you, long before I ever fell for you."

"Make love to me, Jimmy," Corey whispered.

Jimmy leaned over him, pressing his lips against the back of Corey's neck. "We just took a shower."

"We can take another one."

"I just put the cream on you."

"We can get more cream."

"Your back is so sore...."

"Jimmy?"

"Yes, baby?"

"Shut up and fuck me!"

NATE CARTER wasn't hard to find. He had a fan page on Facebook, and Jimmy sent him a private message. Hopefully he'd respond. They also went through the previous five years of the show, looking for every young, boyish-looking contestant.

"It won't hurt to contact them," Corey said. "Even if they are unwilling to talk, at least we'll have tried."

"Yep," Jimmy agreed. "How'd everything go with your ma? I mean, back home before you left, did she come around at all?"

"I haven't talked to her since I moved out," Corey said. "I wonder if she'll even watch the show."

"You know, she can come here if you make it into the top ten. They allow you to have one family member."

"Is anyone from your family coming?"

"Charlie wants to, but I think it'll be my mama. Daddy has to work."

"Who'll stay with Charlie?" Corey asked.

"We haven't worked it all out yet. There's no point worrying about it just yet. We gotta see how I do in the competition. I could be going home in two weeks, ya know."

"I doubt that. If you do make it all the way, though, won't the whole family come out?"

"I think so. I think the show will pay for their trip."

"I'm not sure I'd even ask my mom. Maybe Megan and my sister."

THE contestants were instructed to assume that they'd make it all the way to the end of the contest. The two weeks leading up to the live broadcasts were a time of preparation. Corey rehearsed numerous songs. He was given an itinerary that identified the themes of each week in the competition. For one week they would focus on classic rock, and all of the song choices were required to reflect that theme. For another week it would be country western, and they had a week scheduled to honor Michael Jackson, while another week celebrated Elton John.

Halfway into the second week, Corey was ready with six songs. It was sort of a catch-22. On the one hand, he did not want to be presumptuous. He could not get overconfident and assume that he'd automatically make it through. After all, the American public had not even yet voted a single week. He might not even make it into the Top Ten.

Contrarily, he had to prepare himself. There had to be a certain level of confidence that fed his drive to go on. He had to be able to envision himself as America's Next Superstar. It was like Charlie had said. He had to really want it. And he *did* really want it. He wanted it more than anything, and at times he would find himself so overwhelmed with emotion that he'd start getting choked up for no apparent reason. Being there in Hollywood, preparing for the biggest competition of his life, was the fulfillment of his grandest dream.

It was Saturday morning, and Corey knew the judges would be returning in two days. He'd likely hear again from Reuben. Jimmy and he had been working on a plan, and they had an appointment to meet with an attorney that morning. It was their only option due to the demands of their schedules. Jimmy had found him on the Internet and had already spoken to him multiple times on the telephone. If he couldn't put something together fast, they didn't know what they would do when Reuben returned.

"Mr. Sawyer and Mr. Dunham?" The man who approached them was in his midthirties, dressed casually. Corey had expected some old stodgy guy in a three-piece suit. "I'm Devin Burbank. We spoke on the phone."

"I'm Jimmy, and this here is Corey," Jimmy said. "Thank you for meeting us."

"Not a problem. Thank you for calling me. This is a huge case, and there are a lot of attorneys who'd give their eyeteeth for this kind of opportunity."

"So you believe us?" Corey said.

"Oh, I believe you. I've seen the pictures you emailed me, and I've read the statements from the other boys who were victimized. Before I turn this over to the prosecuting attorney, though, I have to explain some things to you." The boys nodded their agreement. "First of all, I think you may have a civil case against Mr. Jameson, but I don't see where he's committed any crime against you. In legal terms, it was two consenting adults engaging in sexual activity."

"But he forced Corey! He blackmailed him."

"Yes, I know, but Corey is nineteen. If the prosecutor takes the case, Jameson will be charged with statutory rape and child molestation, but the charges will be associated with two of the other victims."

"That's fine," Corey said. "Just so he's charged and can't keep doing this."

"We have their testimonies, but we don't have photos like you provided."

"So it'll just be their word against his?"

"I do think that we may be able to use Corey's and Tristan's testimony to corroborate, though. If so, Jameson is in deep shit."

"Mr. Burbank," Jimmy began.

"Please call me Devin."

"Mr. Devin, I have something else I need to tell you."

He raised his eyebrows and leaned against the table. "Go ahead."

"Reuben has pictures of me… and a video. He was using this to blackmail Corey."

"I don't understand. Why would pictures of you give Jameson any leverage over Corey? Was Corey also in the pictures?"

"We're gay," Corey said, "and Jimmy and I are a couple. We love each other."

Devin nodded. "Okay. Well, how did Jameson get this video?"

"A couple years ago when I was back home in Kentucky, I met a guy on the Internet who said he was looking for models. I talked to him on webcam, and he offered to pay me a thousand dollars to be in his movie."

"An adult movie?"

"Yeah, well, I didn't exactly know what I was getting into, but my family needed the money. He flew me to Los Angeles, I made the movie and took the money. He paid me cash, and I took it back home to my family."

"And Jameson found the video on the Internet?"

"Reuben apparently owns this adult movie company," Corey said. "He had the video already, but supposedly it's never been released. He said if I don't do everything he says, then he will sell the video, kick Jimmy off of the show, and ruin him forever."

Jimmy slid the manila envelope across the table toward Devin. He opened it discreetly and looked inside. "Wow," he said. Jimmy blushed.

"I can't believe you're just now telling me this. I thought Corey was being blackmailed by Jameson by being threatened to be kicked out of the competition."

"We tried to stop Reuben back in New York. He wanted Corey back then, but we threatened to expose him. Tristan was too scared, though."

"You said this video was made two years ago?"

"Yes, sir."

"And you're nineteen now?" Jimmy nodded. "So this is a huge problem for Jameson. There is a reason he never released this video. All of these porn companies—the ones that are legit—are very fastidious about keeping records. They're required to have on file a copy of the ID of every model."

"Yeah, they asked me for a driver's license, and I told 'em I ain't got one. So they made me sign a paper. But I thought the age of consent was seventeen."

"The paper doesn't mean anything. What they probably planned to do was date the affidavit after you turned eighteen and claim that they filmed the video at a later date. If they were audited, they'd have to contact you and get you to send them a copy of your ID. Age-of-consent laws do not apply to pornography. Filming or photographing anyone under the age of eighteen is considered child pornography. It's a felony."

"Really? Well, don't worry, I'm not sending them anything," Jimmy said, shaking his head.

"No, of course not. But these videos are worthless. That right there is another criminal case in and of itself. If you do well in this competition, the publicity could be more damaging to you than if we just dropped it."

"Can you at least get the video?"

"I'll try," he said. "But don't worry about it. Reuben is going to have enough problems to deal with. He's not so stupid that he'd risk being exposed as a child pornographer."

"Devin, what should we do? Reuben will be back on Monday, and I know he's gonna contact me," Corey said.

"Do nothing," Devin said. "Mr. Jameson is bluffing. He can't do anything with this video. Probably the reason he's holding onto it is because he doesn't want it to get into anyone else's hands. He knows the laws. He's known all along that Jimmy was underage. If you get any more notes from Jameson, don't respond to them. If you get any visits from him, ask him to leave, or call security."

"Why don't you just go arrest him?" Jimmy asked.

"That will be up to the prosecutor. They'll need to do a full investigation, which could take weeks or months."

"And in the meantime, Reuben will keep doing this stuff," Corey said, infuriated.

"Well, he can't touch either of you. Is there anyone else in the competition that might be in danger?"

"There are ten other guys," Jimmy said. "Half of us will be voted off next week, though. None of them are the same type as Corey. It seems like all of Reuben's victims have that same sort of look."

"Cute white boys," Devin said.

"Exactly."

"Okay, so I am going to go forward with this and turn everything over to the district attorney's office. You may be contacted by them. If so, call me. Don't say anything to anyone, and if you do get called for questioning, tell them you want your lawyer present."

"Yes, sir," Jimmy said.

"And stop calling me sir," he said with a wink. "My daddy is 'sir'. I'm Devin."

"Yes, Mr. Devin. Sorry."

FOURTEEN

FOR the first week of the competition, there would be three broadcasts. On Tuesday evening, the male contestants would perform. Wednesday would feature the female contestants, and the results show would be on Thursday. The first week was the scariest, because almost half of the Top Twenty-four would be eliminated. The top ten vote-getters would automatically move on in the competition. The judges would select three other contestants out of the remaining fourteen. Those three "wild card" choices would also move on, but the remaining eleven would go home.

Everyone prayed that they would be among the lucky thirteen who were saved. Corey knew that this was the biggest hurdle. To have made it this far in the competition—all the way through the audition process and the New York elimination rounds—only to then be voted off in the first week, would be horrible. But if he were lucky and could make it past this week, Reuben would not be able to touch him. From that point forward, the worst thing Reuben would be able to do would be to offer negative feedback about his performance. The history of the show indicated that the general public did not place much stock in Reuben's critical opinions, though. Often they voted the opposite of how Reuben advised.

"I'm nervous," Corey confessed to Jimmy.

"You're gonna do great. We both are." Jimmy squeezed his hand. They were standing backstage along with the other twenty-two performers but were in the back of the group. At the opening of the show, the entire twenty-four would take the stage for a group song. Corey looked up at a clock on the wall, noticing they were only ten minutes from going live.

"At least he never contacted me," Corey said. "I wonder why?"

"Who cares? It doesn't matter what he does from now on. Just concentrate on doing your best, and he won't be able to touch you."

When Dylan Seagraves stepped into the room, all eyes turned to face him.

"Good evening, Superstars," he said cheerfully. "We're five minutes to airtime. Everyone ready?"

Corey didn't feel ready at all. He'd never performed before such a huge audience. To make matters worse, he knew that he was going to be seen by most of the country and a good portion of the world. He wasn't sure if he felt more like throwing up or passing out.

I'm at home in Mom's bedroom, holding the extension cord in my hand, dancing in front of the mirror. It's just the two of us, Mom and me, and she's so proud of me.

He had to find a way to distance himself from the reality of the situation. He had to carve out a safe mental space for himself, or he'd never make it through.

All my life I've dreamed of only one thing: singing. It is who I am and what I was born to do. From the time I was born, I've lived for this moment... and at last it's here. I know I can do it. I didn't come all this way to fail.

The next thing he knew, the houselights went down and Dylan stepped out on stage into the spotlight. "I'm Dylan Seagraves, and we're here tonight to choose America's *Next* Superstar!"

The theme song for the show blared as Corey felt himself being ushered out on stage. Without thinking, he stepped in line, meticulously following the rehearsed choreography. As the lights shone on him and the other contestants, he couldn't even see beyond the edge of the stage, and he sang the lines he'd memorized. It sort of felt like he was in a trance, but he knew his part so well that it just flowed out of him.

Minutes later, the music had ended. He made it through the opening song and even did well with his small solo. They were now at a commercial break, and the houselights were back up. Quickly the female contestants were directed offstage to sit in a designated section of the audience. The male contestants congregated backstage.

Thankfully, Corey did not have to do his song first. He was scheduled to perform fourth. Jimmy was sixth. The first contestant, a twenty-two-year-old African American named Eli Brown, did exceptionally well. The crowd reaction was thunderous, and all four judges heaped praises upon him afterward. The next two performers didn't fare so well. They both stumbled, and one was even flat throughout his song.

After a second commercial break, it was at last Corey's turn to sing. Dylan introduced him by first showing a brief video of his audition. Corey felt his face redden as he watched himself on the monitor. Then suddenly the intro was over, the lights went down, and the music started. Corey stepped out on stage, exactly as he'd rehearsed, and began to sing.

For that three and a half minute time period, the earth seemed to stand still. Corey felt as if he'd been transported to another plane, and he sang with all his heart. Every note perfect, every syllable of his lyrics crystal clear. The emotion of the song bubbled up from deep inside him as he belted out the lyrics, rising at just the right moment to tackle the climax of the song. When he got to the dramatic finale, the high notes at the end, he nailed them.

Sweating profusely and out of breath, he remained center stage and took a bow as tears streamed down his cheeks. The houselights began to come up, and he saw the entire audience was on their feet—even the judges.

Somehow he'd done it. He'd made it through his performance, and done so flawlessly. Not a single negative comment was uttered by any of the judges, not even Reuben. Raymond even went so far as to proclaim him the "voice to beat" in the competition.

After his performance, he was allowed to take a seat in the audience and watch the remaining performances. There was only one he cared about.

When it was Jimmy's turn to perform, Corey laughed right out loud as he watched his adorable audition tape. That was exactly how he looked that first day they met. He was sexy in his tight blue jeans and T-shirt. His accent seemed so much more pronounced back then. After the intro tape concluded, the lights went down, then suddenly a red spotlight appeared on Jimmy, who was sitting on a stool center stage. He was strumming his guitar.

Corey was pleased that Jimmy had chosen a country ballad. That was definitely Jimmy's strength, and his rich baritone voice was perfect for that type of song. His performance was magnificent. It literally brought tears to Corey's eyes, and of course he felt as if every word of the song was directed right at him personally.

The crowd reaction was almost equal to what Corey had received, but the judges weren't quite as kind. Three of the judges were complimentary, but Reuben raked him over the coals.

"I'm sorry, but it felt very karaoke to me. Very amateurish." The crowd booed Reuben for his negativity. Clearly they loved it in spite of Reuben's mean-spirited remarks.

After the show, Corey and Jimmy shared a limo back to the hotel. Jimmy had the driver stop at a liquor store. Since he wasn't old enough to buy real champagne, he got a nonalcoholic version along with some plastic wine glasses.

"There are wine glasses in the minibar back at the hotel," Corey reminded him.

"I wanted to get something special," Jimmy said. Corey laughed and kissed him. "We have to celebrate."

"How can we celebrate if we don't even know yet if we've won?"

"Because we did our best, and no matter what anyone says, we couldn't possibly do more than that."

They were petting heavily when the limo finally stopped in front of the hotel. "Can't we just stay here all night?" Corey asked.

"You never did it before in the back of a limo?"

"Not yet...."

Just then the door opened. The chauffeur was letting them out.

"We'll have to work on fulfilling that fantasy before we go home," Jimmy said with a wink. He crawled out of the car, and Corey quickly followed. Jimmy's arm was around his shoulder as they walked through the front door and headed toward the elevator.

"We could do it in the elevator too," Corey suggested. "Another unfulfilled fantasy."

Jimmy grinned and then bit his lower lip. "Don't tempt me."

When the elevator door opened, Corey gasped. It was Reuben, standing on the other side of the door. Without a word, he stepped forward and walked right past them. Corey and Jimmy scurried into the cubicle and pressed the button for their floor.

"Weird," Corey said. "He didn't even look at us."

"I wonder if he knows we turned him in."

"Or if he thinks he's just making me sweat," Corey said. "Maybe he's just waiting until he's in the mood to use me again."

"Well, that ain't never gonna happen," Jimmy said. "Unless it's over my dead body."

WHEN Corey awakened Wednesday morning, he felt as if a huge burden had been lifted from his shoulders. He'd made it through the night of competition and had faced Reuben for the first time. The world hadn't come to an end. He felt very confident about his performance, and when he turned on the television set that morning, he started screaming. *The Today Show* was running a clip of his performance.

"What's wrong?" Jimmy came running from the bedroom, wearing only his boxers, sleep still in his eyes.

"They're showing us on TV!" Corey said.

"Oh...," Jimmy said, "I thought it was something important."

"Look! Now they're showing you."

The hosts of the talk show were discussing their favorite performances, and the consensus among them was that Reuben had been far too harsh on Jimmy. They all thought he was spectacular. They only showed a total of four clips, their top picks from the night, and both Corey and Jimmy were among them.

"Jimmy, we're celebrities now. We made it on *The Today Show*."

Jimmy turned around and stumbled back into the bedroom. "Congratulations," he muttered as he slipped back into bed. Corey barely noticed Jimmy's lack of enthusiasm. After finishing his cup of coffee and surfing the channels to see if there was any other news about the show, he slipped back into the bedroom himself.

Very carefully he pulled up a corner of the bed coverings and crawled between the sheets, positioning himself so that he had full access to Jimmy's midsection. When he fished inside the fly of Jimmy's boxer, unwrapping the prize inside, Jimmy moaned and rolled over onto his back.

"Jimmy Sawyer, you party pooper, you're gonna have to work on being a better morning person. Maybe I just need to give you something to smile about." He then wrapped his mouth around Jimmy's throbbing morning wood and didn't come up for air until Jimmy was writhing on the mattress and bucking his hips.

When at last Corey threw back the covers and emerged to Jimmy's smiling face, he knew he had accomplished his mission. "That's better," Corey said with a satisfied nod. "Good morning."

"Morning," Jimmy echoed, a broad grin on his face. "What was that for?"

"You were being grumpy," Corey said, sprawling out across Jimmy's chest. He nuzzled his face into Jimmy's neck.

"Mmm, do you promise to do that every morning I'm a grouch?"

"I'll do that anytime, anywhere you want it...."

He felt fingertips gliding gently up the sides of his torso. "Baby, I love you," Jimmy whispered.

"I love you too, Jimmy Sawyer... my Superstar."

It was an hour later that they finally climbed out of bed together.

"WHAT'S going on out there?" Corey asked the desk clerk as he pointed to the front entrance. Security guards were stationed at the front door as a mob of onlookers crowded next to the building.

"You're a celebrity now," the young lady replied. "Those are all fans. They're gathered outside hoping to see the *Superstar* contestants."

"Really?" Corey gasped. "How will we get through that mob?"

"You're going to have to plan everything from now on," she explained. "If I were you, I wouldn't count on being able to just take a casual stroll down the sidewalk. If you want to go somewhere, you'll have to arrange transportation."

"Ain't that something?" Jimmy said, scratching his head. "We thought it'd be a relaxing day. We were just gonna go for a walk."

"I'm sorry, Mr. Sawyer," the clerk said. "But if you'd like, I can call a cab or limousine for you."

"You can call me Jimmy," he said. "I think maybe we should just stay in for the day."

"But this is our only day off," Corey protested. The girls would be performing tonight, and all the focus was now upon them. That gave the male contestants a break for one day.

"We can go to the gym together," Jimmy suggested. "Then we'll have lunch and watch soap operas in our room this afternoon. We won't even have to leave the hotel."

Corey made a face. "You hate soap operas," he pointed out.

"You two are real cute together," the girl said. Corey looked at her nametag.

"Thanks, Katrina," he said. "Did you watch the show last night?"

"Oh, yeah. You both were great." She leaned slightly over the counter, lowering her voice. "And I voted for you both—ten times apiece."

"Really?" Corey said. "That's really sweet."

"It's cool how you two are such close friends. Is it hard? I mean, you're competing against each other?"

"You're not the first one to ask that," Corey said. "But no, it's not hard at all. It really doesn't feel like we're even in competition. We both want the other to do well."

"Can I ask you something?" she said.

"Sure."

"Are you two... ya know... um, a couple?"

Corey looked at Jimmy before answering. "We aren't here to make any kind of statement. We're just trying to win a contest."

"Oh... I know, and I'm sorry. I didn't mean to be nosy. It's just that my brother is gay. It would be so cool if a gay guy won the competition. It'd mean a lot to him, and to a lot of other people."

"You tell your brother we're just like him," Jimmy said, his voice ringing with confidence. "Please, don't broadcast it, though. Technically we're all supposed to be virgins."

"It's in the contract," Corey explained. "Romances of any kind are forbidden."

Katrina started laughing. "That's such bullcrap. There are all kinds of romances every year. People love that kind of stuff. But don't worry, I won't blow your cover. Just be careful, though. From now on, you won't have much privacy. You don't really have to worry about the hotel. We're very strict about keeping the media and fans out unless they have permission. But once you walk out those front doors, you're an open target."

"Thanks, Katrina," Corey said. "It's great advice."

"Can I ask one more thing?"

Corey smiled and nodded.

"Can I have your autographs?"

"WE'RE gonna have to be careful," Jimmy said. It was Thursday morning, and the boys were having breakfast together in Corey's room.

"What do ya mean?"

"Well, we both know that Reuben wants to get rid of me, right?"

"Probably both of us," Corey said, taking a bite of his toast.

"I don't think so. He sees me as the instigator. I'm the one who challenged him, who kept him from you and who interfered with his involvement with Tristan. He voted against me when they chose the Top Twenty-four, and he's always made nasty comments about my performances."

"Okay, I see your point. But why's that mean we have to be careful?"

"You know the rules, Corey. Contestants are not allowed to be romantically involved with each other."

"But he already knows. I think everyone knows. How can they not?"

"That's not the point. Everybody knows that gay people are everywhere, especially in the music industry. Officially, the policy is that they don't discriminate. But even though they have this nonfraternization policy, they turn a blind eye to the straight couples. They have an image to maintain, though, and if a gay couple were exposed, they might not tolerate it."

"So you think they might kick us out at this point? Don't you see that as being a much bigger problem for them in the long run? If they kicked us out for being gay, the whole country would turn against them."

"Well, probably not the whole country, but it would be a lot of really bad press. They wouldn't kick us out for being gay. They'd say it was because we broke the rules. They'd call it a sex scandal."

"That's such a double standard," Corey said. "They never kick out the straight couples who are in the tabloids every year."

"And I really don't think they'd want to do it to us either. I'm just sayin' that it is something that Reuben could use against us if he chose to. I mean, if he wanted to get rid of me bad enough, he could bring us both down. I think that right now he's very motivated to keep you in the competition. Corey, he wants you."

"Then why hasn't he contacted me?"

"I bet he will. It's just a matter of time."

"And then what? When I refuse him, maybe he will try to kick us out."

"Let's just hope that Devin's able to convince the prosecutor to move quickly."

COREY had never been able to dress this nicely. He'd never purchased a pair of designer jeans or even an expensive pair of shoes. He prided himself on always looking fairly fashionable, but it was fashion on a budget. For the first time in his life, he was dressed to the nines. He stood there in the dressing room, examining his reflection. The sport coat alone probably cost as much as his mom's secondhand car.

Well, this was it. The moment of truth had arrived, and he would find out for the first time what the American people thought of him. He'd been following his website, the one that the social-networking specialists had designed for him. It had gotten more than seven million hits since Tuesday. His fan page on Facebook had 300,000 followers. The only thing he didn't know was how many of those fans would vote for him.

Standing backstage next to Jimmy, he couldn't even hold his hand. The cameras were on them because the show was about to start. All the contestants smiled, many of them waving, as the camera panned the group. Suddenly the lights dimmed and the theme music started. Dylan Seagraves took the stage and delivered his trademark introduction. The first song of the evening was performed by a former *Superstar* winner. When she was finished, the twenty-four contestants were introduced.

"Tonight we'll be announcing America's Top Ten, and in addition, the judges will choose three wild-card picks."

Corey stared out into the audience, noticing that many of the fans were holding up placards and posters declaring support for their favorite contestants. He saw a couple of signs with his own name and tried not to smile.

"Please dim the lights as I read the top ten," Dylan went on.

Corey was glad that this part of the show presented quickly. He hated it when they drew it out into a long ordeal. Generally they tried to make it as dramatic as possible, and waited until the last five minutes of the show before delivering the final results. On this particular episode, though, they had to announce the top ten first, and then the drama came in with the selection of the wild card picks.

Corey's knees nearly buckled when he heard Dylan call his name. He was the very first contestant chosen! He turned to Jimmy and grabbed hold of him, hugging him tightly.

"Congratulations," Jimmy whispered in his ear. "I knew you'd make it."

Corey was instructed to step over to the side of the stage and take a seat on one of the benches that had been set up. After seven more names were called, Corey was starting to sweat. There were only two more chances for Jimmy to be called. The seriousness of the situation suddenly hit him. What if Jimmy got voted off? How could he possibly go on without him? What would he do about Reuben, and how could he make it through the upcoming weeks on his own?

Most of the contestants had family members. If their families were not there in person, they at least were able to call home. Corey was pretty much on his own. Plus, he knew how much the competition meant to Jimmy. He knew how unselfishly Jimmy had lived his life. He'd done everything for his family, and his very motivation for being in the contest was to provide for his family and to make his brother proud.

"Elaina Covey, you are in the top ten!" Crap, that only left one slot. This was Jimmy's last chance to be selected. If he didn't make it, he'd have to earn a wild-card slot, and that was not likely—not with Reuben as one of the judges. The wild-card slots were chosen by unanimous vote. The four judges had to decide upon three contestants they all agreed deserved to move on.

"And America, your last top-ten contestant for this year's *America's Next Superstar* is... Jimmy Sawyer!"

Corey shot to his feet and began applauding. So did the rest of the auditorium. He could see the relief wash over Jimmy as he doubled over, burying his face in his hands. It was all Corey could do to avoid bursting into tears himself. As Jimmy headed over to the benches, Corey stepped out and hugged him, patting him hard on the back.

"I was so scared," he whispered.

Jimmy looked at him and smiled, tears streaming down his red cheeks.

FIFTEEN

THE first four weeks of the competition went much smoother than Corey would have predicted. For one thing, they were all extremely busy, and the days seemed to fly by. The elimination rounds were stressful, but Corey knew that both Jimmy's and his performances were strong. They were stronger than several of the other contestants, and it was no real surprise to see some of the others get voted off.

It got scary after they got down to the top eight, and Corey started to feel as if any one of them could be voted off. As he watched some of the other performers, he began to realize that this really was a competition. They all were very talented, and all it would take was a single screwup to ruin everything.

Corey stopped worrying about Reuben. He did have to deal with him that one night every week when he offered his critique of Corey's performance, but for the most part he was complimentary. He continued to degrade Jimmy, but the audience had grown used it, and Reuben's snarkiness had little impact.

Each week when Dylan announced the results of the nationwide vote, he'd begin by forming a group which he called the "Bottom Three." These three were the lowest vote-getters for the week. At the end of the show, he'd bring the Bottom Three center stage and inform one of them that they didn't make it through, and he'd tell the other two that they were safe.

So far, neither Corey nor Jimmy had been in the Bottom Three. Corey was relieved to learn that once again he was safe and had avoided elimination. To his horror, though, Jimmy was announced as one of the Bottom Three.

It was just like the first week of the competition. The same fears washed over him, and he sat there literally trembling. *Please let Jimmy be safe! Oh, God, please.*

Thankfully, Jimmy was indeed safe, and made it through for at least another week.

"If I made it into the Bottom Three, that means there's a chance I could go home soon," Jimmy said.

The two of them were in bed together. "Jimmy, don't say that. Big deal, out of eight people, you came in third from the bottom. You had a bad week. Your song choice didn't really fit you, but you're super popular. Have you looked at your website lately?"

"I try not to look," Jimmy said. "I got to stay focused on this here. I can't go worryin' about what people are sayin' on the Internet."

"I'm just saying, you have a lot of fans, and they're gonna keep voting for you."

"Well, I just hope I can make it through next week. Mama and Charlie are coming. It'd be real disappointing to be voted off in front of them."

"I'm so glad they worked it out so that Charlie could come too."

"Did you call your mom?" Jimmy asked.

Corey shook his head. "Megan said she won't even answer her phone."

"Really? I hope she's all right."

"Well, I guess I've become kind of a celebrity at home too. Every week they have big parties at the bowling alley where they watch *Superstar* on the big screen, and then everyone votes for me afterward."

"Aww, that's kind of sweet."

"Yeah, well, Mom apparently got tired of people calling all the time and unplugged her phone."

"Call her cell phone, then," Jimmy suggested.

"She has a cell, but only uses it in the car for emergencies. She's really old-fashioned when it comes to technology."

"Sounds like my granddad."

COREY was awakened the next morning by the phone. "Hello," he said, his voice groggy from sleep.

"Mr. Dunham, there is a gentleman here to see you. He says he's from the prosecutor's office."

"Oh... okay, wow. Um, does he want to come up to my room, or am I supposed to meet him downstairs."

"He says he will come up."

"Okay, give me like five minutes... uh, please."

Corey hung up the phone and turned to Jimmy. "Quick, get up. The prosecutor is here to see us."

About ten minutes later, the three of them were sitting in the living room.

"This is going to be a tough case," Mr. Roberts informed them. He was a slender man with gray hair. "Jameson is going to have a team of defense attorneys, and this whole thing's gonna be a media circus."

"Will we have to testify?" Corey asked.

"At some point, if it goes to trial."

"What do you mean, *if* it goes to trial?" Jimmy asked. "Why wouldn't it?"

"Jameson has a lot of money. Often in these cases, the molester will offer a huge cash settlement to the victims to keep them quiet. Without their testimony, we have no case."

"Even if you subpoena them?" Corey asked.

"If they recant their testimony, there's no point."

"That sucks!" Jimmy said.

"Are you aware if Jameson is molesting any other boys at this time?" the prosecutor asked.

"We don't know. We haven't heard from him... other than on the show."

"Okay, well, I think the best course of action is to sit on this for a few more weeks. We'll wait until the end of the season and arrest him after the last show."

"But why?" Jimmy asked. "You know he's guilty. Why don't you go after him now?"

"Because of the media. It would be just crazy right now, and it wouldn't be good for either of you. You would be right in the middle of what the media would label as a scandal. Just concentrate on finishing out the competition. During the last week of the show, we will issue an injunction preventing Jameson from leaving the country."

"But then he'll know...."

"Yes, and he'll most likely gather a team of defense attorneys. That's why we don't want to move on this until right before we're ready to make the arrest."

"And what about Corey in the meantime?" Jimmy asked. "You're leaving him a sitting duck."

"No, if Jameson makes any more moves on Corey, call me right away. We'll intervene. Hopefully that won't happen."

"I don't like it," Jimmy said. "Reuben could show up here at Corey's room any night, and he'd be defenseless."

"Don't you share this room with him?" Roberts asked.

"Not officially."

"Well, I suggest you stay here as often as you can."

Corey smiled as he looked over to Jimmy. *At least now we have an excuse. We have to sleep together by order of the cops.*

THE next week, both Corey and Jimmy made it through easily, with neither being in the Bottom Three. Their schedules started to become busier because in addition to the competition itself, they were required to make numerous media appearances. On some days, they interviewed on talk shows. They were featured in television commercials. Jimmy made an appearance on *The Tonight Show with Jay Leno*, and Corey was on *Ellen*. Corey's very existence changed. He was no longer able to be anonymous. He couldn't so much as go out for a burger or visit a shopping mall.

For three more weeks, they continued to sail through in the competition, and there were then just four contestants remaining. The two other contestants were a male and a female, and Corey knew that in all likelihood it would be a male contestant who was voted off. He feared it would be either him or Jimmy. After this week's show, the three remaining contestants would be sent home for four days. These homecomings were a trademark of the show. Huge events were planned, including a parade and an enormous concert.

Corey honestly was not overly excited by the prospect of returning home. He had no idea how his mom and sister would receive him. The whole thing would be awkward if none of his family even showed up. He did want Jimmy to get his big homecoming, though. He knew it would mean a lot to him. He was already a hero in his hometown. It would be just devastating for Jimmy to be voted off at this stage and not get his parade.

The four contestants stood together on the stage, locking arms around one another's shoulders. No matter which of them went home, it'd be sad. Corey had grown to love his competitors—though none as much as Jimmy—and he knew it would be tough to say goodbye.

"Dim the lights!" Dylan declared dramatically. "Jimmy Sawyer, you sang 'We Danced'. Raymond felt it was your best performance yet. Krystal said you gave her goose bumps. Tyler said it was a beautiful performance and that you owned the stage. Reuben felt you fell flat. But what did the American people say? With a record thirty-two million votes, Jimmy Sawyer, you are... *safe*! You're headed back to Kentucky for a grand homecoming and a final victory lap before our big finale."

Corey's heart soared, thrilled Jimmy had made it.

"America," Dylan said, "this is your Bottom Three this week. Two of these contestants will go on. All three of them will go home after the show tonight, but only two will return to compete next week."

He then went through the recap of each of their performances, once more paraphrasing the critiques they'd received from the judges. "Elaina Covey, you are safe!"

Corey's heart pounded in his chest. It was down to just him and the other contestant, Curtis Wang. Curtis wrapped his arm tightly around Corey's waist as they stood there, and for a moment Corey feared he would pass out. "Corey and Curtis, only one of you is going through to the next round. The other has reached the end of your journey on *Choosing America's Next Superstar*. Corey Dunham... you've made it through! You are safe! I'm sorry, Curtis, you did not make it."

Corey immediately turned to Curtis and pulled him into a tight embrace. They were both crying. "Congratulations," Curtis said. "You really deserve it. You're one of the nicest people I've ever met."

After ten long weeks it all came down to this. Both Corey and Jimmy had made it through. In two more weeks, one of them might be America's Next Superstar. Or it could be neither. But for now, it was time to head back home. For four long days, he and Jimmy would be separated. Although it'd be hard, he knew it was something that Jimmy would love. He was so close to his family, and Corey sort of wished he could just go with Jimmy back to Kentucky and completely forget about his own homecoming.

"I'm gonna miss you," he whispered into Jimmy's ear, later, as they cuddled in bed together for the last time before their departure.

"We'll be back here before you know it," Jimmy assured him.

"I'm glad you get to fly home with your mama and Charlie."

"I'm sure there will be lots of people in Michigan waiting to see you," Jimmy assured him. "Maybe you can talk your mama into coming back with you."

"Maybe," Corey said, unconvinced. "It'll be nice to see Megan again, and Lanie."

"And when you come back, I'll have a surprise for you," Jimmy said.

"What do you mean?" Corey smiled at him as he ran his hand across Jimmy's smooth, hard chest. "I don't want a surprise when I get back. I want it now."

"Too bad," Jimmy said, his expression smug.

"That's not fair!" Corey protested, grabbing hold of one of Jimmy's nipples and tweaking it.

"Hey! That hurts!"

Corey leaned over and kissed the exact spot he'd just tortured. "Please tell me now," he pleaded, lapping Jimmy's sensitive nipple with his tongue.

"No! That ain't gonna work!" Jimmy bolted from the bed.

"Aw, come on," Corey looked up at him with pouty eyes and a protruding lower lip.

Jimmy shook his head. "I said it's a surprise. Deal with it."

THE biggest surprise of all was the crowd that greeted Corey when the limousine drove him into his hometown. About a mile outside of town, the police were waiting for the limo, and they escorted Corey into the downtown area. The chauffeur opened the sunroof, and Corey was instructed to stand on the seat so he could stick his upper body out and wave to the crowds. He'd never seen so many people in his town. There were thousands upon thousands lining the streets, all of them waving and cheering, holding signs in his honor.

"Oh my God!" he cried. He couldn't believe it. The whole thing was absolutely crazy. It felt more like he was some kind of war hero than just a shy kid who'd entered a talent competition.

The limo drove him straight downtown to the big park next to city hall. A huge crowd had gathered, and a special path had to be cleared for the limo. They drove Corey right up to the steps of the band shell where he'd be performing. As he stepped out of the vehicle and climbed the stairs, all he saw was an enormous sea of faces. There were so many people there, all of them applauding, many shouting out how much they loved him. He suddenly was again overwhelmed by a wave of emotion. He nearly stumbled going up the steps, unable to see through his tears.

"Thank you so much," he said into the microphone, his voice cracking. "I can't believe you all came. I just can't believe it." He then turned, and saw his mother standing to his left. "Mom!" he cried. She stepped over to him and embraced him.

"I'm so sorry," she said into his ear. "I'm just so proud of you, baby."

He kissed her on the cheek and then pulled her once again into his chest. "I love you, Mom."

"I love you too."

His little sister Lanie was also there, and so was Megan. He hugged and kissed them, and then noticed some of his coworkers from the supermarket.

In spite of Corey's misgivings, the homecoming had been a huge success. He felt so welcome and so proud of his accomplishment, while at the same time humbled by all of the attention.

Later, after all the musical performances and speeches, Corey went home with his mom and sister. Megan came over to the house as well. Corey was toting a box that contained an array of trophies and plaques that he'd been awarded. He got a key to the city, a gold-plated plaque from his employer, a framed letter from the governor, and a lot of other souvenirs from fans.

"Can you guys go back with me?" Corey asked. "You wouldn't believe it. I've got a huge suite at the hotel. The show will also pay for your own rooms. I can bring my whole family if I want...."

"What about my job?" Corey's mother asked.

"Mom, can't they give you the time off for something like this?"

"Mrs. Dunham, Corey is famous now. He's going to be very wealthy... even if he doesn't win the competition. He can help you with your bills."

"I'll pay them all off!" Corey said excitedly. "I've already had record companies call me, offering me contracts."

"Really?" she said.

"Mrs. Dunham, didn't you see all those people? Corey is a superstar now. Everyone in the whole country knows who he is."

"And now they'll know who you are too," Corey joked. "You'll be on TV too."

"You mean... I might not have to worry about this mortgage?"

"Mom, fuck the mortgage! I'll buy you a new house."

She was so happy that she didn't even scold him for swearing.

COREY'S entire outlook changed while home. After the warm reception he received, he was relieved and felt unburdened. His estrangement from his mother and sister had weighed heavy on his heart, and now he felt free. A part of him worried that his mom still might not accepted him for who he was, but it was a step in the right direction. At least now she was ready to meet Jimmy, and she'd accepted that he was a big part of Corey's life.

It seemed as if the outcome of the competition was inconsequential. It was odd, because Corey had worried all along that if he and Jimmy both made it to the very end, they'd face a terrible conflict, but he didn't feel the least bit competitive. He was at peace with whatever decision the voters made. Regardless of which of them won the competition—or even if neither did—they could both come away from the experience deeply enriched.

Corey flew back to California on Tuesday, and his mom and sister followed the next day on a commercial airline. He'd been texting Jimmy over the past four days, and they'd spoken a few times on the phone. Jimmy's homecoming was all that Corey's had been and more. As he sat in the limo on his way back to the hotel, he sent Jimmy one final text, letting him know that he was back.

Jimmy responded, saying he was in his own room, and that he wanted Corey to meet him there. Corey expected that it was because Jimmy's family was with him. It'd be good to see them all again. When he got back to his room, the bellhop deposited his bags inside the room. After tipping and thanking him, Corey decided to take a quick shower. He wanted to look and smell his best when he saw Jimmy and his family.

Ten minutes later, with a towel around his waist, he stepped out of the bathroom and headed into his kitchen area to grab a bottled water. He stopped dead in his tracks when he noticed an envelope on the floor by the front door. He knew exactly what it was—another note from Reuben.

Corey rushed over and picked it up. He wasn't going to let this ruin anything. The lawyer and the prosecutor both had told him not to respond to any contact from Reuben. He tossed the letter, unopened, on the bureau and headed back to his bedroom to get dressed.

When Corey arrived at Jimmy's room, he knocked and waited for the door to open. He didn't have his own key because they'd never stayed in that room. Jimmy had always stayed with him. Thirty seconds later the door opened, and there Jimmy stood, more striking than Corey had ever seen him. Jimmy was dressed to the nines, decked out in a formal tuxedo.

A huge smile erupted across Corey's face. "I think I'm underdressed," he confessed.

"You're perfect," Jimmy said. He held out his hand and escorted Corey into his room. The lighting was subdued, and the room was accented with candles. Soft, romantic music was being piped in, seemingly by magic.

"What's going on?" Corey asked.

"I told you when you got back I'd have a surprise," Jimmy said.

"Room service? A tuxedo? Jimmy, this is amazing... you've planned a romantic evening for us."

"Yes, I have, but that's not the real surprise," he said. He walked Corey over to the sofa and motioned for him to sit. Stepping behind him, he gently began massaging Corey's shoulders. "How was your flight?"

"It was fine," Corey said. "I knew I was coming back to you."

"I missed you."

"I missed you too... so much!"

Jimmy bent over and kissed the side of Corey's neck. "You smell good," he said and then moaned. Jimmy then stepped around to the front of the sofa so that he was standing before Corey. He lowered himself, bending one knee.

"Corey, I love you with all my heart," he said.

Corey raised his hand to cover his mouth. He couldn't believe what was happening. It was beyond his wildest dreams. "Oh, Jimmy," he gasped.

Reaching into the pocket of his jacket, Jimmy pulled out a small box and held it in his hand. "I don't want to go on with my life unless you're in it," he said. "You're the fulfillment of my every dream. Corey, no matter what happens in the contest, I want us to stay together. I want to wake up with you every morning. I want to come home to you every night. I want to make a life together... grow old together."

Tears streamed down Corey's cheeks as he looked into Jimmy's chocolate-colored eyes.

"Corey Dunham, will you marry me?"

Corey began to nod, biting his lower lip to keep from completely losing it. "Yes!" he cried. "Oh, God, yes!" Jimmy removed the ring from the box and slipped it on Corey's finger.

As Jimmy pressed his lips against Corey's, delivering the most searing and passionate kiss Corey had ever experienced, Corey melted into Jimmy's embrace. Soon Corey felt himself being lifted by Jimmy's strong arms and carried into the bedroom. They made passionate love several times. Three hours later, exhausted, they returned to the living room and ate their cold supper.

"I'll order us some hot food," Jimmy said.

"No, this is fine," Corey said. "It's perfect."

Corey didn't bother telling Jimmy about the letter he'd received. It didn't matter. They could deal with it in the morning. Tonight was too special, and Corey wasn't going to let anything ruin it.

SIXTEEN

IT WAS going to be a big day for both Corey and Jimmy. Not only were their families arriving that day, but it was also a performance night. Only three contestants remained in the competition—Jimmy, Corey, and Elaina. Conventional wisdom was that Jimmy and Elaina would be the most vulnerable for elimination. They were both country-western singers, and it wasn't likely they'd face off against each other in the final round. On the other hand, Elaina was the only female, and that factor could be detrimental to Jimmy and Corey.

"Either way you look at it, I'm at risk," Jimmy said. His tone was lighthearted, and he made the comment with a shrug. Corey suspected that he had pretty much developed the same attitude that Corey had. They both felt as if they were already living their dream. They'd already been blessed beyond measure, and they'd gladly accept their role in either first, second, or third place.

When they headed over to Corey's room that morning, Corey decided to inform Jimmy about the letter. "Reuben sent me a letter last night," he said, trying to sound casual.

"What?" Jimmy stopped walking. "Corey, why didn't you tell me?"

"I dunno. Just didn't want to spoil our night. Besides, at this point it doesn't matter what he said."

"Let me see it," Jimmy said, holding out his hand.

"It's in the room, and I haven't even opened it."

Jimmy rushed along down the hallway, hurrying to get to the room. Once inside, he spotted the envelope on the bureau. He picked it up and tore open the envelope, reading it aloud.

"If you don't want your friend eliminated tomorrow, be at my room at midnight."

Jimmy tossed the letter back onto the stand and pulled out his cell phone. He first called his lawyer and then the prosecutor.

"Do they think he's bluffing?" Corey asked.

"Yeah, but what Devin is worried about is the possibility that Reuben could leak the pictures to a third party and have them post them on the Internet. We could still go after him in a lawsuit, but that wouldn't stop him from getting me kicked out."

"Oh my God! Why is Devin telling you this now? He should have mentioned that a long time ago. I never thought about that—"

"They're probably going to arrest Reuben today," Jimmy interrupted. "They wanted to wait, but after this, they think it'll be a lot of publicity for us no matter the timing."

"Oh God… and my mom's coming today. She's gonna find out about Reuben and what I let him do to me."

"It takes a while for all the facts to come out in these cases," Jimmy explained. "The big news today will just be that Reuben's been arrested. I'm sure he will be out on bail within hours. He might even be on the show tonight."

"Are you serious?"

"I don't know. A person is innocent until proven guilty."

"Unless you're the victim," Corey snapped back.

Jimmy nodded. "It doesn't seem fair."

"Anyway, we have a rehearsal in an hour, then our families will be here this afternoon. The police are gonna do what they need to do, and we've got to go on with our own business."

"Exactly. Unless I hear otherwise, I'm gonna act as if I'm still in the competition."

AFTER rehearsal, Corey rushed back to his room and turned on the television. He surfed the channels, checking all the news programs, and there was nothing about Reuben. He then checked the Internet. About a half hour later, Jimmy arrived.

"Have you heard anything?" Corey asked.

"Nothing." He shook his head.

"I just got a text from Lanie. They arrived at the airport about ten minutes ago and will be headed over here. She'll text me when they arrive, and I'll go down to meet them in the lobby."

"Daddy, Mama, and Charlie are already here," Jimmy said. "Maybe we can get everyone together for a few minutes this afternoon."

"Should we tell them anything about Reuben?"

"No, let's wait."

JIMMY went downstairs with Corey to meet Corey's mom. It was the very first time they'd met. It came as no surprise to Corey that Jimmy was very polite and charming, and Corey sensed that his mom really did like him.

A few minutes later, they met Jimmy's parents in the hotel restaurant. Everyone was hugging each other and interacting as if they'd known one another for years. About halfway through the meal, Charlie spoke up, asking Corey a question.

"Where'd you get that rock you're wearing?" he said. He was referring to Corey's ring.

Corey looked at Jimmy, not knowing whether he should go ahead and answer the question, or leave it up to Jimmy.

"Corey is engaged," Jimmy said proudly. "We're getting married."

Mrs. Sawyer gasped, jumping up from her chair to embrace her son. Charlie and Lanie were smiling and laughing, congratulating them. Charlie reached over to pat Corey firmly on the back, and Lanie came over to hug him. Only Corey's mother and Jimmy's dad remained seated, not really saying much.

Finally Mr. Sawyer spoke. "Son, I'm so happy for you, and very proud. Have you decided where you're having the ceremony?"

"Well, we have to go to a state where it's legal to get our license… but we are thinking of having a big ceremony back home."

"Does this mean you're leaving Michigan?" Corey's mom asked.

"Probably," Corey said, reaching over to take hold of her hand. "But we'll talk about it. It's not something we're going to do immediately. I'd like you to think about maybe moving closer to us."

For the remainder of the meal, they talked about nothing other than the wedding. Mrs. Sawyer was thrilled and rattled off a litany of ideas about the cake and the tuxedos and which church they'd use. Corey couldn't believe how open and accepting Jimmy's family was. Never once did they say a single word about it being a gay wedding.

Oddly, neither did Corey's mother. But Corey suspected she was thinking thoughts like that. He feared that on the inside she was far more uncomfortable than she was letting on. It seemed ironic to Corey that this traditional family from Kentucky was so accepting and welcoming, while so many other people in his life struggled.

"Isn't your friend Megan coming out?" Jimmy asked Corey.

"If I make it through this week, she will come out for the last show."

"Well, one thing's a guarantee. Either you or I will make it through," Jimmy said.

"Both of you will make it through," Charlie said confidently. "You're both better than that girl."

"We'll see."

IF THEIR performances were any indication, Charlie was right. Each of the contestants had to sing two songs that evening. Both Corey and Jimmy's were spectacular, and one of Jimmy's songs was dedicated to his brother. There was hardly a dry eye in the auditorium.

Reuben had not been arrested. He remained in his normal judge's seat and said all of his typical sarcastic remarks.

After the show that night, both families gathered in Jimmy's room. Everyone was excited, confident that they had both given amazing performances and had an excellent chance of making it through to the final round.

"There's something that Corey and I have to talk to y'all about," Jimmy said. He seemed to quickly revert to his full accent when his family was around. "It's something I'm not real proud of, but I'm afraid pretty soon you're gonna all find out."

Jimmy glanced over at his father and then back down at the ground. "Remember a couple years ago when Charlie had one of his surgeries? We needed money real bad, and I got an advance at work?"

Mr. Sawyer nodded. "Yes, son, we will always remember the sacrifice you made for our family."

"Well, it wasn't exactly an advance."

"What do you mean?" Mrs. Sawyer asked. She and her husband were sitting on one of the sofas. Jimmy and Corey were on the floor, sitting beside each other.

"I met this guy on the Internet, and he paid me to be in a movie." Jimmy's voice began to crack, and Corey reached down to grab hold of his hand. "I'm sorry," Jimmy said, attempting to regain his composure.

"What kind of movie?" his mother asked, her voice barely above a whisper. She had to know what Jimmy was talking about but just didn't want it to be true.

"The kind you're probably thinking of," Jimmy said.

"Jimmy!" Charlie cried. "Why?"

"Like I said, I wasn't proud of it."

"You did that to get money for our family... because of me." Charlie buried his hands in his face and began crying. Jimmy slid over to his brother and embraced him.

"Son, what does this mean?"

Corey spoke this time. "It doesn't really mean anything. Jimmy was still a minor. That movie can never be released." He then went on to explain how Reuben had been trying to blackmail them. The hardest part was telling his mother about what Reuben had done to him.

"Why isn't this man in jail?" Corey's mom asked.

"We don't know," Jimmy said. "We thought he'd be arrested today."

"He'll get away with it," she said. "He's rich and famous, and he'll get the best lawyers."

"But, Mom, if they do arrest him, this stuff will probably all come out in the news. It'll be a huge scandal, and Jimmy and I will be right in the middle of it."

"What about that movie? Can't they kick you off the show for that?" Mrs. Sawyer asked.

"I think it depends whether or not they can keep that part of the story out of the media. The big scandal is going to be what Reuben did to all these other boys. If Corey and I are dragged into it at all, it'll be to testify."

Corey was surprised by how well everyone took the news. His mother was visibly disturbed when he explained that he'd been abused by Reuben, and Mr. Sawyer said he wanted to kill the bastard. But nobody said anything negative about Corey or Jimmy, and when they all went to bed that night, Corey felt relieved and unburdened. He was glad the truth was completely out in the open, and no matter what happened from that point forward, he knew he'd have the love and support of his family.

JIMMY'S cell phone woke them up the next morning. "Hello," Jimmy croaked into the receiver. Corey lay there, half awake, trying to decipher who Jimmy was talking to.

When he ended the call, he explained to Corey that it had been their attorney. "They cut some kind of deal with Reuben," he said.

"What?" Corey couldn't believe what he was hearing. The news was incredulous. "How? Why would they do that?"

"He got the tape and all the photos from Reuben, and they aren't going to press charges on the child pornography. They're going to charge him with child molestation, but he has until the day after the competition to turn himself in. They want to do it quietly, avoid a media circus."

"So we're gonna have to face him?" Corey sat up in bed, shaking his head. "He knows we're the ones who turned him in, and we have to perform again in front of him?"

"Well, at least one of us does," Jimmy said. "Maybe both."

"If they were going to do it this way, why didn't they just wait?"

"They had to get the video. By cutting this deal with him, they were able to get the video into their hands before he destroyed it."

"I'll be so glad when this is over!"

"It may not be over for a long, long time," Jimmy said. "And I bet Reuben tries to pay off the witnesses."

"Maybe he'll at least be kicked off the show," Corey wished out loud.

THE show that evening was incredibly emotional. They showed footage of each of the homecomings. Seeing it all capsulized into a five-minute video was even more moving than living through it. As thrilled as Corey was to see his own video, he was equally impressed with Jimmy's.

Jimmy's homecoming event had been held at the fairgrounds, and the place was packed with thousands of fans, all chanting his name. He took the stage and brought Charlie up with him. Charlie stood there while Jimmy sang the song to him that he'd written for him.

At the end of the two-hour program, Dylan Seagraves again had the contestants take center stage. Corey's heart was beating so fast he thought it would thump right out of his chest. They had placed Jimmy and Corey on the outside, sandwiching Elaina between them.

"Dim the lights, please," Seagraves shouted. "Corey Dunham, it's been a long journey for you. We watched you in Detroit as you gave your audition." Behind them, on a big screen, they were showing scenes as Dylan was talking. "And since that point, you never once were in the Bottom Three... until now." The crowd laughed. "But that, of course, is because there are only three contestants left. Corey, they say all journeys must eventually end, and tonight... is not quite the end for you! You've made it through to the final round!"

The entire audience was on their feet, cheering and wildly applauding. Corey was instantly overcome with emotion. He hugged both of the other contestants, and then stepped to the side of the stage to await Jimmy's fate.

"Not since the very first season of *America's Next Superstar* have two male contestants squared off in the final round of competition. This could be another year like our first. *Or* we could have a battle of the sexes.

"Jimmy Sawyer and Elaina Covey, both of you have come a long way. Both of you have had incredible journeys, and as we saw in your homecomings tonight, you've both made your hometown communities proud. But only one of you can go on to compete in the final round.

"Dim the lights please. Elaina and Jimmy, for one of you, your journey has come to an end. Sadly, the contestant who will go home tonight *is....*

"Elaina Covey. Jimmy Sawyer, you are going on to the final round of competition!"

It was like something right out of a fairy tale. How could it even be true? Both he and Jimmy had made it all the way through, and one of them would be America's Next Superstar!

It was a long, joyous night. After the show, the two finalists had to meet with the press for photos. They were grilled with questions, hugged, photographed, congratulated, and praised about a million times. It wasn't until after one in the morning that they made their way back to the hotel.

SEVENTEEN

SIX days later, Jimmy and Corey competed against each other one last time on the *America's Next Superstar* stage. It had been the most grueling week of rehearsals that Corey had endured thus far. They were singing three songs apiece, and Corey wanted to do something fresh. He had a repertoire of songs to choose from, but he needed at least one of his songs to go outside the box.

He decided to sing one song that would be significant to Jimmy and him, and so he chose a country classic, "When You Say Nothing at All." The song seemed perfect, especially because Jimmy was so often a man of such few words.

His other two choices were pop songs that had originally been sung by boy bands. Corey had always liked that style of music, particularly because the members of those groups were generally such strong vocalists. They had to be. When those groups were formed, only the most powerful and perfectly pitched voices were chosen, and the resulting harmonies were beautiful.

Jimmy went 100 percent country in his performance. One of his songs was a bit more upbeat, but the other two were heart-rending ballads. These were Corey's favorites, actually, and they almost always brought tears to his eyes. He was glad Jimmy selected the songs that he did, and he knew that Jimmy had at least an equal chance of winning.

After the show, nobody dared predict who the winner would be. They'd all have to wait until the next night, Thursday, when the results were announced at the end of the season grand finale.

It felt good to be finished with the competition. There'd be no more performances other than a couple group songs they'd be singing at the beginning of the final show.

"Good luck tomorrow," Corey whispered as he snuggled against Jimmy's warm body. They were in bed together.

"You too, baby."

"You realize this is our last night together," Corey said. "Whoever wins tomorrow will be flying to New York, and the other is going home."

"We won't be separated for long," Jimmy said.

"I know, but I'm not looking forward to it."

Corey relaxed, resting his head in the crook of Jimmy's shoulder, and slowly drifted off to sleep. All his life he'd dreamed of being America's Next Superstar, but as he closed his eyes, he prayed a silent prayer. *Please, God, let Jimmy win. He deserves it so much more than me.*

The show was broadcast live at eight o'clock Eastern time, which meant it started at five. They took a limo over to the theater to rehearse one last time with the group, and when they were finished, Corey realized it was only one in the afternoon.

"You know, I think I might go home and take a short nap. I'm really exhausted."

"Okay," Jimmy said. "You sure you're not hungry? We could grab lunch."

"I'll get a bite before I come back over at four. What are you gonna do?"

"I think I'll call my folks and see if they wanna meet me."

"Good idea."

When Corey got back to his room, he called the front desk and asked for a wake-up call at three o'clock. He then sprawled out on the sofa and drifted off. A few minutes later he was awakened by a knock on the door.

He was confused when he first woke up, not used to sleeping in the afternoon. But he stumbled over to the door and flung it open. There before him stood Reuben, and Corey's jaw nearly hit the floor.

Reuben didn't wait for an invitation. He stepped into the room, pushing his way past Corey.

"What are you doing here?" Corey asked. "You're not supposed to...."

"I won't be at the finale this evening," Reuben said. "I just met with the producers and tendered my resignation, effective immediately."

"Reuben, I don't care. After today, I never want to see you again. Now if you'll kindly leave, I won't have to call Security."

Reuben took a step closer to him. Corey felt his heart rate quicken. The last time he was alone in a room with this man....

"I'm not here to hurt you, Corey. I never meant to hurt you."

Resolved to show no fear, Corey took a deep breath and looked Reuben right in the eyes. "You have a funny way of showing it, Reuben. What you did to me... it was sick."

"What we did together was beautiful," Reuben said, his voice thick with emotion. "Don't belittle it. Don't turn it into something obscene."

Corey couldn't believe what he was hearing. "You tied me up and tortured me," he said.

"Corey... my sweet innocent Corey, we made love. We made beautiful love."

"Reuben, you're sick. I don't care what kind of shit you're into. If you wanna play around with bondage and domination—whatever your thing is, I couldn't care less. But when you force it on someone else, that's not making love. That's *rape*!"

"You were so pure, so perfectly innocent and undefiled." It was as if Reuben was in a world of his own. The man had not heard a word that Corey said. "And so utterly helpless."

"Reuben!" Corey screamed. "Listen to me! I'm not helpless, and I'm not innocent. Don't you realize I'm the one who turned your ass in?"

"No… no, no, no… it wasn't you. It was that other one. The other one I liked, at first. He's the one who corrupted you."

"Jimmy?"

"Yes, Jimmy. He was the other one I'd chosen. It was supposed to be the three of you. The one who looked like Justin Bieber."

"What are you talking about?" Corey yelled. "Do you mean Tristan?"

"Tristan, Corey, and Jimmy. You do realize that if I had not handpicked you, none of you would have made it through auditions. And Tristan, that boy was just exquisite, my absolute favorite."

"What happened? What was it that changed?"

"They all change," Reuben said, his voice very matter-of-fact. "They lose their innocence. The fear and panic eventually leaves their eyes as they grow accustomed to the things I do to them."

"And then you have to either intensify the torture, or move on to your next victim," Corey whispered. It all was starting to make sense. "And when you found the video of Jimmy, you no longer had any interest in him. He'd already been corrupted. The only victims you like are virgins… or at the very least, they must seem like virgins."

"And now it's over," Reuben said. "Now everything has been ruined."

Corey took a step back as he noticed the rage in Reuben's eyes. Reuben reached behind him and pulled something out of his waistband. A knife!

"Reuben, no! Please.…." Corey took another step back.

"You and your friend ruined everything. You've destroyed my life!" Reuben lunged toward him. Corey spun around, barely avoiding the trajectory of Reuben's swing. As Corey's body twisted, he stumbled, falling flat on his face.

Reuben dropped down on top of him, flipping him over and pinning him to the ground. Corey was terrified, but the weight of the bigger man atop him had him trapped. Reuben used his knees to pin Corey's arms against the floor, and then he pressed the knife against Corey's throat.

"Don't make a sound," Reuben threatened.

Corey wanted to scream for help, but he knew it'd do no good. He'd be dead before anyone heard him. "Please, Reuben," he pleaded. "Please don't...."

The door behind them suddenly flew open. "Freeze, police!"

It was Mr. Roberts, the prosecuting attorney, and he was accompanied by two officers. Reuben dropped the knife and raised his hands in the air. Seconds later, Corey was back on his feet, and Reuben was facedown on the floor with his wrists cuffed behind his back.

"We've been monitoring the security cameras in your hall for the past several weeks," Roberts explained.

Corey was trembling, and tears were flowing freely down his cheeks. One of the officers led him over to the sofa. "Can I call Jimmy?" Corey pleaded.

The district attorney nodded. "Go ahead."

IT WAS almost four thirty when the police car dropped Jimmy and Corey off at the back of the theater. They raced inside and headed straight for the dressing rooms.

"Where have you been?" one of the producers shouted.

"Sorry," Jimmy said. "Long story."

"Hurry!" she said. "Makeup! Wardrobe! Get over here, stat!"

Thirty minutes later the boys were standing just offstage waiting for the show's opening number. Jimmy took hold of Corey's hand. "Are you okay?"

Corey nodded. "I am now."

"I'm so proud of you," Jimmy said. "You were very brave, the way you stood up to that maniac. I'm sorry I wasn't there to protect you."

"Let's not talk about that man anymore," Corey said. "He's hurt enough people, and he can't hurt us anymore."

The grand finale show was absolutely amazing. Famous musicians from around the world, people Corey had only dreamed of ever meeting, were there to perform. Not one word was said about Reuben's absence. It was as if he was never even a part of the show. Corey should have been on pins and needles. He should have been obsessed over who would win the competition. But inside he felt very calm, and he wasn't worried at all.

The show lasted for three hours, but it wasn't until the very end that Dylan had Corey and Jimmy take the stage one last time.

"Ladies and gentlemen," he began, "America has spoken. You have selected your next Superstar, and I have the results in my hand, right here in this envelope. Dim the lights, please!"

"Corey Dunham and Jimmy Sawyer, one of you is America's Next Superstar." Dylan peeled open the envelope and pulled out the card inside, reading it and then nodding.

"And the winner is… Jimmy Sawyer!"

Immediately the crowd erupted in uproarious cheers, confetti fell from the ceiling, and Jimmy was surrounded by people. Tears streamed down Corey's face as he looked over at him, thrilled beyond words. His man had won. Jimmy had made it all the way, just like Corey knew he should, and he didn't feel even a tiny bit of regret or jealousy.

Jimmy pushed his way through the throng of people, as microphones were shoved into his face. He grabbed hold of Corey and hugged him tightly. "I love you," Corey said into his ear. "Congratulations."

Jimmy pulled back, but only briefly, and then, on live international television, he leaned in and gave Corey Dunham the most passionate kiss of his life.

And Corey felt like a Superstar.

JEFF ERNO works a full-time job as a retail store manager, and at the age of thirty-seven, he finally acquired his bachelor's degree in business management. He began writing in the early 1990s, primarily as a means of catharsis after having experienced the multiple losses of several close family members and friends. Originally his work was posted on a free amateur website, where it was eventually discovered and published.

Erno currently resides in southern Michigan with his twenty-one-year-old cat, Winston, and he co-owns a book review website that focuses on M/M fiction. He enjoys reading, movies, theater, country-western music, community service, political activism, and cake decorating.

Visit his website at http://www.jefferno.com.

Also from JEFF ERNO

WE DANCED

JEFF ERNO

http://www.dreamspinnerpress.com

Also from JEFF ERNO

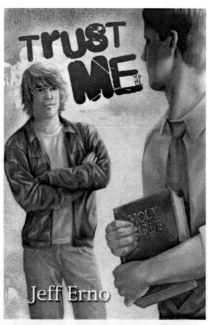

http://www.dreamspinnerpress.com

CPSIA information can be obtained at www.ICGtesting.com
Printed in the USA
LVOW130636170912

299067LV00002B/9/P